Josie's Handyman

Josie's Handyman

RENIE SMITH

RESOURCE *Publications* · Eugene, Oregon

JOSIE'S HANDYMAN

Resource Publications
An Imprint of Wipf and Stock Publishers
199 W. 8th Ave., Suite 3
Eugene, OR 97401

www.wipfandstock.com

PAPERBACK ISBN: 978-1-7252-7760-1
HARDCOVER ISBN: 978-1-7252-7761-8
EBOOK ISBN: 978-1-7252-7762-5

Manufactured in the U.S.A.   08/07/20

This book Is dedicated to my son, Dan Smith,
who encouraged me to find a publisher;
To my dear friend, Laura Collins,
for all of her proofing, questioning and evaluating
and to Jim Beaird for his editing assistance.
I love you all.

Chapter 1

Scott looked over the job application in his hand. "Josie. Isn't that a girl's name?"

"Named for Josie Wales."

"Josie Whales?"

"Wales. Guess you're not an Eastwood fan then?"

"Oh, yeah. I remember. An outlaw or something, right?

"Yeah. The Outlaw Josie Wales. My dad is a major Eastwood fan."

"I'm not much into westerns," Scott replied.

"Guess that shoots any chance that you're a John Wayne fan then?"

"Well, the Duke is in a class by himself. I like him a lot."

"Good. I was starting to worry about you." Josie almost smiled.

"Yeah. Well, about your references here, all right if I call any of these?"

'Well, sure. Wouldn't do me much good if you couldn't, would it?"

"Guess not. How about if I make a couple of calls and then give you a call later this afternoon? You going to be around?"

"Sure. I've got my cell with me so whenever. . ."

Josie walked to the pickup and swung up. Fastening her seatbelt, she started up the motor and eased out into traffic. That didn't look like a bad shop to work out of and Scott seemed nice and knowledgeable enough. I'll have to thank the guy at the gas station for the tip. He said Scott is a friend of his. She and Scott had talked shop a half-hour or so before the discussion about her name. That was close. She hadn't wanted to lie. Trying to keep her voice low was enough of a strain. Remembering to do it was even worse.

1

Josie Elliott didn't usually tell half-truths or even total untruths. But she knew she'd never get a job as a handyman here in South Dakota, or anyplace else, if they knew she was a woman. The fact that she'd worked with her dad all through high school, taken several shop courses from a local vocational school and then worked full time with her dad, who was a building contractor, wouldn't be enough. Men just didn't think females could do certain jobs. The contractors in Montana who'd rejected her without even acknowledging her credentials had proven that.

The references wouldn't betray her gender. They were friends and working associates who knew what she was capable of. They'd tell the truth about her work but that would be it. They'd all tried to talk her out of this 'foolish scheme' as they put it but promised to let her do it on her terms. She hadn't asked them to lie about anything. Just not to let it slip that she was a girl.

Josie found her motel on Mt. Rushmore Road and decided to risk a swim in the pool. It was hot and she doubted anyone would notice her.

IN THE SHOP SCOTT hung up the phone. Both references on Josie had checked out and had even given him more info. This guy really sounded experienced and Scott could do with some good luck. The last guy he'd hired had stolen something from the home where he'd gone to repair the back step. He shouldn't even have gone inside the house. Fortunately, the homeowner had noticed the missing watch right away and the local police had found the 'handyman' before he could skip town. Scott knew his insurance would have covered the watch, but nothing can undo the bad word of mouth, especially in a small town like Rapid City, SD. The customer had accepted Scott's apologies and statement that the man had been immediately fired. Of course, they had been customers for various repair jobs over a few years, so Scott had somewhat of a relationship built up with them. That helped. So did the fact that they all went to the same church.

JOSIE WAS JUST TOWELING herself off from her hurried swim when her cell phone rang. The call was local, so she figured it was about the job application and lowered her voice as she answered the phone. She couldn't help but smile as she hung up. She could start Monday. That gave her Friday and the weekend to find a rooming house or small apartment or whatever—just so it was furnished.

Once in her room, she even did a little 'dance of joy'. Dressing again, in her 'guy clothes' she left to purchase a newspaper. Back in her room she scoured the ads for a place to hang her hat, at least temporarily. Scott had told her that this was the middle of 'tourist season' here so motel rates were not available as weekly or monthly like you would find in the off season. She found a few rooms listed and called each one. Two were already taken, one wouldn't be available until Sunday, but she could go by and take a 'peek' and another sounded great but came with a rather high price tag. She went to 'peek' and gave the owner the first week's rent. Moving in Sunday afternoon would be fine. She didn't have that much stuff with her. If she really liked it here and decided to stay, she'd have her dad ship more of her stuff from Montana.

WHEN JOSIE WALKED INTO Scott's shop Monday morning, he showed her a clipboard with several orders for work. He started to give her directions to the first one when the phone rang again. Holding his hand up to tell Josie to wait, Scott found himself on the other end of a frantic, nearly hysterical customer. Seems the kitchen sink was shooting water all over the place. Scott didn't usually take regular plumbing jobs, he left that to the local plumbing shops, but the customer said he'd called several and no one could get there before Tuesday afternoon. Covering the mouthpiece, he explained quickly to Josie and at her nod, he told the customer Josie would be right over.

"Don't know for sure what you're walking into on this one, Josie. I'm sorry to start you out like this. But you're up on plumbing enough, you think?"

"I'll see what the deal is, at least get the water shut down, and then we can decide from there." Josie replied.

"Thanks." Scott explained how to get to the address and Josie hopped in her pickup and headed out. Yes! She was officially on the job and had an assignment. Rapid City wasn't a large city so, even though she was new to town, Josie found the address easily. The man who opened the door looked like he'd taken a shower with his clothes on.

"Come in, please," he said, grabbing her arm and pulling her toward the kitchen. "Careful. Don't slip."

It took all of her self-control not to laugh out loud. Water was shooting every direction from the faucet. It was running down the walls, pooling on the floor, and dripping from the ceiling. A woman was frantically mopping but was clearly losing the battle.

"Okay, Mr. Browning, what started the flood?"

"Well, I bought a new faucet and was going to install it myself." He looked rather sheepish. "It didn't sound all that hard. But before I could even get the old faucet off, this started."

"So, you didn't shut the water off before you started?"

"That's what the directions said. But it wasn't on. Helen had just washed the dishes and then turned the water off."

"You needed to turn the water off at the shut off, where it comes into your house. That way there won't be any in the pipes to gush out when you remove the faucet. Now, where's your shut off?"

"Shut off? I don't know. We've never had to shut it off. Helen, do you know where the water shut off is?"

"How would I know?" his wife snapped, still mopping as fast as she could. She was filling a bucket and then emptying it elsewhere, probably in the bathroom, Josie guessed. Poor woman looked like she'd about had it.

"Okay. Where is your water meter?"

"Water meter? Well, I don't know. Where do you think it might be?"

Josie was really struggling not to laugh. It wasn't funny to these poor folks, but she could hardly wait to call her dad and tell him about this one.

"The meter reader has to come every month to read the meter. Does he come inside?" Josie asked.

Helen nodded. "There's a couple of those guys who come around and they always go downstairs." She opened the door to the basement and flipped on a light. Josie ran down the steps and looked to her right and then her left. There was the meter and, right above it, the shut off. She twisted the valve to the right until it was tight.

As she ran back up the stairs, she heard the customer and his wife yelling that the water had stopped shooting out. They were so grateful to her for stopping the flooding that she almost didn't know what to say to them. She explained that once the new faucet was on, they should turn the water back on but to go slowly in case there was a leak. Then they could shut it back off and get everything fixed before they turned the water on again. She almost asked if they just wanted her to put the new faucet on for them but decided that wasn't her call.

Using the cell phone Scott had given her she dialed the shop and explained the situation very briefly and asked how he wanted her to charge for the call. Laughing, Scott said to just charge the minimum and come back in. Josie wrote up the ticket, accepted the customer's check, and headed back to the shop. She laughed most of the way there, knowing she couldn't laugh much with Scott or he'd be able to tell that she was a girl.

"Wow! What a first day!" Scott was laughing so hard he couldn't answer the phone when it rang. He just handed the phone to Josie and went to the pop machine. After he took a drink of his soda, he wiped his mouth and forehead with his sleeve.

Josie took the phone number of the customer calling and promised to have Scott call them as soon as he returned to the shop. Lying wasn't her forte but she realized that Scott truly couldn't talk at the moment.

He was still laughing. "Sorry. But that's the funniest thing I've heard in a week of Sundays."

"Yeah! I had an awful time keeping a straight face. It looked like something out of the 3 Stooges or something. I can't wait to call my dad. He'll fall down laughing. But those poor people were certainly not amused."

"I'm sure they weren't," Scott said. "Well, here's the next job. This is a duplex and the kids living in the other side punched a hole clear through the sheet rock on both sides of the dividing wall. Owner says he'll evict them but right now the couple in the first side has a toddler that wants to crawl through the hole to the other side. For some reason," Scott grinned, "the mom doesn't want him to do that!"

"I guess there'd be insulation there?" Josie queried.

"Yeah. Actually, that's why the mother is so upset. The little guy started pulling it out and made a real mess. Plus, she knows there's stuff in it he shouldn't be messing with."

"I'll just take a sheet and cut to fit. You got a bucket of mud?" Scott pointed to a large bucket and showed Josie some smaller ones to use to go on the job. Josie slapped some into the smaller bucket, grabbed some tape and a piece of sheet rock and headed out the door to her pickup. Coming back in to grab the tools she'd need she asked Scott about the paint. "Are they just going to paint this when it's dry or do I schedule some time tomorrow to go back and paint?"

"The owner said he'd take care of the paint. He did all of the painting and has the matching leftovers."

Josie nodded and climbed into her pickup. Scott had given her a page to track her mileage, as he'd be paying her for using her own pickup. She jotted down her mileage, checked the city map, and pulled out into traffic. She liked driving her own vehicle but she kind of wished it were a company truck with the business information on the door. Then when people saw her driving, they'd know she was officially an employee of Scott's Handyman Service. Oh, well. She knew. If those Montana contractors could just see her now. She grinned.

SCOTT WATCHED HER GO. There's something about this guy I can't put my finger on. Seems nice enough, doesn't talk a lot, doesn't smile or laugh often. But I know he was totally tickled about the waterfall this morning. He shook his head. Everyone is different and if the guy does his job well, that's all I can really ask.

"IT WAS SO FUNNY, Dad," Josie gasped. "I laughed so hard going back to the shop it's lucky I didn't run into someone or something."

"What did your boss say?"

"He laughed too. In fact, I had to take a call for him because he was laughing so hard, he couldn't talk."

"What's he like? You going to like working for him?"

Josie told her Dad all she could about Scott but realized she didn't know much about him. He'd kept her busy all day and showed her a full clipboard for tomorrow. He worked on various jobs in his shop so he could handle the phone. He seemed to be quite a good carpenter as he was building a chest of drawers for a customer and Josie thought it was very nice. "He does nice work and adds little touches that make the projects special. I think he really enjoys what he's doing."

"That's nice, Josie. I'm glad you found someone to work for that you can get along with."

"Dad! Are you saying I'm hard to get along with?"

"You know better than that! But sometimes perfectly nice people just don't see eye to eye. That makes for long days at work."

"I know, Dad. I was just joking."

THE WEEK HAD GONE by quickly and Josie found it difficult to believe that it was Friday already. Scott paid by the week, so she'd get a paycheck on Monday for this first week of work. It would really be official then.

She still didn't know much about Scott, but she'd paid closer attention since speaking with her Dad. Just what kind of man was Scott Mayforth? He wasn't wearing a wedding ring and she'd never heard him mention a wife or girlfriend. Actually, he didn't talk about much except work.

Oh, yes. Something else she'd noticed. She'd never heard Scott swear or use foul language. She'd heard plenty of rough talk when she worked with her dad. His employees watched their tongues, at his request, but other contractors had often gotten quite foul. A couple of times her dad had talked to them and asked them to respect his daughter's presence on the job. One had said that if a girl couldn't handle the job environment, she should find a kitchen someplace to take refuge in but mostly, after her dad mentioned it, the guys toned down their language. And the dirty jokes. That was even worse. Hmm. She hadn't heard any of that from Scott either.

What kind of guy is he? Does he have family here? Did he grow up here? What does he do when he isn't at work? Funny, he doesn't seem like a close-mouthed kind of guy but I sure don't know much about him.

As SCOTT LOCKED UP the shop Friday night and headed home to change clothes and get to his church league softball game, he found his mind drifting back to his new employee. He did every job I sent him on with no complaints. When I went by to check his work on a couple of jobs, I had to admit I couldn't have done better myself. But why does this guy seem like such a mystery? Other than the fact that his dad is a contractor, I don't know anything about Josie.

Chapter 2

JOSIE WALKED INTO THE shop Monday afternoon a few weeks later. It had been a busy day but she would now collect her fourth paycheck. She couldn't completely hide the grin that brought to her face.

"Hey, Josie. What's the joke?" Scott looked up from his workbench and smiled. "You look like you just solved the world's greatest mystery."

"Nothing. Just thinking that I've already been here a month."

"Yup. I thought about that last night when I was doing my books for the week and writing your check." He handed Josie her paycheck. "Hope you're planning to stick around for a few more."

"Thought I might." Josie folded her check and put it in the chest pocket of her coveralls. "Thanks."

She turned to leave but stopped when Scott spoke again.

"Hey, man, you been up to Mt. Rushmore since you been here?"

"No. We came through here when I was just a kid and we went up then; I was thinking I'd get back up there one day soon."

"Well, Friday's the 4th of July."

"Yeah. I was going to ask you about that. We closed?"

"Sure are. I don't work any weekends or holidays. Life's too short."

"Cool." Josie nodded.

"Anyway, my family always has a big get together on the 4th. We eat about noon then head up to Rushmore to get a spot where we can see the fireworks. Want to tag along?"

"That's nice of you Scott, but I don't want to horn in on a family thing." Josie shook her head.

"Naw. It's not just a family deal. My sister will drag at least one of her giggly girlfriends along and my brother will have either his latest girlfriend or one of his buddies. My older sister, Brenda, is married and will have her husband and their little boy. But I warn you, we can get loud." Scott grinned. "But we always have a good time together."

"Wow. You have siblings! I've never heard you mention any family. Figured you just crawled out from under a rock." Josie joked. "I'm impressed. Real live relatives!"

"Yeah. Like you ever talk about your family, either. Anyway, you want to come?"

"Can I let you know tomorrow?" Josie asked.

"What? Want to see if you get a better offer?" Scott teased. "Yeah. That's fine."

"Thanks."

As JOSIE DROVE HOME, she tried to figure out how she could go and enjoy the 4th of July with Scott's family without betraying her gender. Obviously, she couldn't go in shorts and a short-sleeved shirt. Jeans? They'd have to be pretty baggy. She turned the wheel and headed for the mall. What she could figure out, clothes wise, would determine her answer to Scott.

Finally, in a pair of men's jeans, with suspenders to keep them up, and a western cut long sleeved shirt worn untucked, Josie's reflection in the mirror said she could, possibly, be a guy. But was it sure enough to risk it? She left the items with the clerk and said she wanted to do a bit more shopping and would bring all of her choices back to that cash register to pay. As she wandered around the store, she mentally rejected every other possibility she came across. After two trips through the store she gave up and returned to pay for her items.

Back at her rooming house, she took her work clothes from today and washed them along with the new items. If she did this every night, she might succeed in taking a little of the 'new' out of her purchases.

DRIVING TO WORK TUESDAY morning, Scott wondered what Josie would say about the picnic and fireworks. I really hope Josie will come. He seems to have made no friends or even acquaintances. He must be lonely. I ought to invite him to church. Hmm. Suppose he'd come?

Wonder what he actually looks like? His hair always hangs over at least half of his face. Scott chuckled. Almost as bad as my sister, Brenda, who is just a little worse than her husband. You'd think they were ashamed of their looks or something. Brenda sure doesn't have to hide her face, she is very pretty. As best I can remember, all the way back to their wedding, Lance wasn't an ugly guy either. But that was about the last time I've actually seen Lance's face. Brenda always had her hair in her eyes. I never could understand how she could see what she was doing. Oh, well. Personal choice. At least if Josie comes to the 4th of July shindig, he'll feel at home.

As JOSIE DROVE TO work, she was still undecided about the picnic. What I can get by Scott, him being a guy, might be a totally different thing from what his mother and sisters would pick up on. What'll I do if they call me on it? Maybe they'll be too nice to say anything to me but they might say something to Scott. What'll I do if he asks me? How could I explain? Would it matter? Now that I've worked for a while maybe he'd be willing to keep me on. Pulling into the shop yard she hesitated before getting out. What should she tell Scott?

ON FRIDAY JOSIE PULLED into the shop yard and saw that Scott was already there. She would ride with him to his family's 4th of July party. She really would prefer to follow him so she could leave if things got uncomfortable, but she couldn't figure how to get that past Scott.

Here goes, she thought as she climbed out of her pickup and locked the door. Scott motioned her over and she got into his truck and closed the door. It felt like she was closing her coffin. She quickly rolled the window down for some fresh air. It didn't really help. She took a long, deep breath and tried to focus on whatever it was that Scott had just said.

"Josie? You okay?"

"Who, me? Sure, I'm fine. Why?"

"Nothing. I thought you just looked a little rattled. My mom always says I imagine stuff." Scott laughed.

"So, tell me about your mom," Josie asked.

"My mom?"

"Yeah. You know. The one who changed your diapers, cooked for you, stuff like that."

"You are nothing but a smart mouth, you know that, Josie?" Scott laughed. "I do know who my mom is. I just didn't know you wanted to know about her."

"Well, I'm about to meet her, right? Thought it would be nice to know what to expect."

"I've yet to see her mistreat a guest, if that's what you're worried about."

"You are absolutely no help, Scott." Josie shook her head. Guess it's a 'guy thing' she thought. Oh, no. What if I gave myself away by asking? I've got to be more careful.

"What's your dad do?" she asked, instead of pursuing the topic of his mother.

"Dad's retired but he was a full-time general contractor. That's where I learned the business."

"Wow. Same thing with my dad except my dad isn't retired yet."

"Yeah. I remember you saying that when we talked the first time. Do you also have brothers in the business?"

"Nope. Just a sister who's in college." Josie grimaced, thinking of what her sister, Hope, would say if she knew what Josie was doing. She was such a prim and proper lady all the time that she didn't even own a pair of jeans. The closest thing to casual wear for Hope was her soccer uniform. Wonder what Hope would think of Scott. Josie turned her head slightly so she could really look at Scott. Yup. Hope would think he was a 'hunk'. Josie had been so worried about maintaining her 'guy' image that she hadn't really looked him over. He was an extremely good-looking guy. 'Cleaned up good' is what Hope would probably say. Josie grinned. Somehow, I'll have to take some pictures so I can show Hope, someday when I dare tell her what I've done.

"Well, looks like everyone's here," Scott said as he pulled up in front of a large, colonial style home. "Come on, let's go eat!"

"Wow. What a pretty house," Josie said. "Your dad must spend hours on this gorgeous lawn!"

Scott looked at Josie a little sideways. "Hmm, I'd never have guessed that you'd get so excited about some green grass."

"Dad has always worked like a slave on our lawn. That may have been the first thing I ever learned." Josie hoped she sounded casual enough. I almost did it again. Of course, a guy wouldn't have said what I did. How stupid can I be? This is going to be harder than I ever thought.

"Come on, Josie. I promise no one will eat you!" Scott coaxed.

Josie shook herself mentally and strode to Scott's side. "Okay. Let's go."

Jim and Barb Mayforth couldn't have been nicer to Josie and she soon felt right at home. She had to remind herself to be careful and not get too comfortable with these people. Scott's oldest sister, Brenda, and her husband, Lance, were also very welcoming. Their little boy, Robbie, was three and an absolute doll. She barely caught herself from saying that out loud. She wanted to squat down and give him a huge hug but reminded herself to stick her hand out and say, "Hey, Robbie, give me five!"

Robbie's huge grin as he slapped her hand just about undid her. He was so cute! Might she have one like this someday? In her dreams!

"We see works!" he said. She looked at Brenda for the interpretation.

"We're going to see fireworks," she explained.

"Yup, Robbie. We'll see fireworks," Josie agreed.

Just then Terry came up to slug his brother in the arm. Ouch. Why did guys have to do that?

"So, Terry, who's your friend?" Scott asked, motioning to the guy hanging back a bit from Terry.

"Oh, yeah. This is Parker, better known as Pegs."

"Pegs?"

"Yeah. Long story," Pegs replied, offering no further explanation.

Scott just shrugged his shoulders and offered his hand to Pegs who shook it like it was the greatest pleasure he'd ever experienced. Scott had trouble getting his hand released from Pegs and wondered if he'd ever get circulation back to his fingers. He shook his hand, rather wildly, and watched Pegs' face start to turn red.

"I'm sorry, man," Pegs said. "I keep forgetting."

"Hey, it's okay. Forgetting what?"

"My brother and I always elbow wrestled and a good hard grip on the other guy's hand is a good start. But I need to remember that not everyone wants to wrestle with me," Pegs explained.

"No problem," Scott said. "Hey, Cindy, it's about time you got up," he greeted his younger sister. "Come on over and meet Josie."

To Josie Scott said, just loud enough for Cindy to hear, "Watch out. No single guy is safe around this one." Then he ducked as his sister took a playful swing at him.

"Did you say Josie?" Cindy asked.

"Yeah. I'm named after Josie Wales." Josie explained.

"Oh, your folks must be Eastwood fans," Cindy exclaimed. "Cool!"

Josie lifted her eyebrows a bit, looked at Scott, and said, "Well, someone in your family knows Clint Eastwood."

"Yeah, yeah. I'm the one who's not up on western movies," Scott muttered. "Hey, Cindy, no boyfriend coming today? That's not like you at all."

"Cody was going to come but we had a fight last night, so I told him I didn't want him here. Now, with Josie here to entertain, it's probably just as well."

"Uh-oh, Josie. Remember what I told you. Run for your life if you have to but don't let her get her hands on you. You'll be ruined, your life over."

"Oh! You are such a jerk, Scott!" Cindy fumed. "If it would do any good to tell Mom, I would."

"I'm a big boy, now, Cindy and I have my own place and business, so I don't think Mom is going to get too upset with me." Scott taunted her. "But, go ahead if you think you still need your mommy to protect you."

Cindy stormed off toward the house, throwing Scott dirty looks over her shoulder as she went. Scott just grinned. "She'll be back in less than five minutes, all sweetness and light," he predicted. "She adores me!"

"Yeah, I could tell," Josie agreed. "So much that if she'd had a loaded gun, I think your short life could easily have come to an end."

"Naw. Her bark is much worse than her bite," Scott asserted. "She misses me if I don't come around often enough to pick on her."

Josie wondered. Cindy had really seemed mad when she left, although Josie didn't think Scott's teasing had warranted such a serious reaction. But out of the corner of her eye, she saw Cindy headed back in their direction.

"See. What'd I tell you?" Scott gloated. "She's crazy about me!"

Josie just shook her head. Is this what it would have been like to have a brother? Not sure this was an experience she really felt deprived of, she watched to see how the next round would go.

Jim and Barb both started calling for everyone to come and eat. Scott said, "Let's go! Mom thinks if we don't come immediately that we're not hungry and then her feelings are hurt."

"Don't want to start off on the wrong foot, do we?" Josie replied as she headed in the direction of the food. "Come on, whatcha waiting for?"

This is what a guy would do, right?

After eating enough food for two or three days, at least, Josie didn't know if she could still move. She was used to usually skipping breakfast, packing or buying lunch every day, and eating her evening meal at her rooming house. This was the best food she'd had since she left home this last time.

Now they were stuffed into three cars for the ride up to Mount Rushmore. She was dying in the jeans and long-sleeved shirt and she had finally given up and rolled up the sleeves; it helped, but not a lot. This was a perfect day for shorts and a tank top or tee shirt, and she envied Cindy and Brenda.

She was riding with Scott, Brenda, Lance, and Robbie in Lance's little Kia. Robbie had started out chattering but had quickly fallen asleep. Brenda was hoping he'd sleep all the way up there. "Then he'll make it through the fireworks. But if he doesn't get a good nap, he'll get too tired and either miss the fireworks or make it miserable on the rest of us."

Josie said she couldn't imagine him being that much of a problem, but Brenda assured her that, without his nap, he was a shoo in for 'grumpy child of the year.'

Josie wondered what it would be like to have a child like that who was totally dependent on you. Sounded kind of nice but even more, it sounded scary. She guessed she wasn't ready for motherhood yet. Good thing. She almost chuckled out loud. Since she was supposed to be a guy she certainly shouldn't be thinking of motherhood.

SCOTT STOLE A GLANCE at Josie and wondered what was going through his head. He sure keeps his feelings under wrap. Wonder if that's how his dad is? There's something about this guy that bugs me, but I sure don't know what it is. Cindy had joked with him and he'd seemed okay with that. But when she started to flirt a bit, Josie had backed way off. Cindy had looked puzzled. Scott grinned. Probably the first time that ever happened to her. Sure hope it doesn't traumatize her too much, he thought.

THE VIEW AS THEY drove to the national monument had been gorgeous, but now the road was getting pretty curvy and the traffic was getting slower and slower. Josie noticed both Scott and Lance trying to peer around the line of cars and wondered if this indicated a problem. "Is it always this busy on the roads up here?" she asked.

"We may not have left the folks' house in time. Looks like we're getting tied up in the traffic we usually beat here," Scott explained. "Means we might have to park and walk quite a ways."

"How many people come up to this celebration?" Josie asked.

"Several thousand. And there will be thousands more that you'll never see who have found spots throughout the hills to park, picnic, and watch the fireworks," Lance said. "You can actually see the fireworks from quite far out."

Scott's prediction soon proved true as they parked the three cars in spaces far apart and quite a distance from the Monument. Grumbling a bit, everyone grabbed chairs, blankets and coolers and started the uphill trek. Despite the size of the crowd, there was still a long time before the program would actually begin but good spots to view the fireworks from would be at a premium so they climbed as quickly as they could. Josie lucked out and didn't get so loaded down she couldn't walk. She feared that, thinking she was a guy, they'd really pile the stuff on her, but they apparently chose to not overburden their guest. She was grateful.

When they were finally settled into a spot Scott asked Josie if she wanted to walk up to the viewing level and get a better look at the faces.

She did and they started up the Avenue of Flags.

"Wow! I didn't remember them this big!" Josie said. "Maybe we didn't get this close when we came before."

"If you really want to appreciate how big they are you should see some of the pictures of men on scaffolding working on them. The perspective is amazing!" Scott exclaimed. "Wanna go inside and see the films and pictures?"

As they looked at various pictures and viewed the video, Josie was overwhelmed. "I can't believe all the work they did and the primitive equipment they used," she remarked. "Bet you couldn't do it today without having to have a terrible amount of insurance just in case someone got hurt and you got sued."

"Yeah. Today's society is always looking for someone to blame for any little thing that goes wrong. Heaven forbid we all be accountable for our own actions." Scott sounded disgusted.

"I know what you mean," Josie agreed. "There are obviously situations where someone was hurt because someone else behaved irresponsibly or hatefully. But so many times, it's just an accident that could have happened to anyone, but you know someone will file a lawsuit."

"Yeah," Scott agreed. "And the cost goes up for everyone in the country to pay for it."

As they turned back to the books and pictures of the actual carving of the four huge faces on the granite rock, their conversation turned back to more pleasant topics. Josie wished she had a camera and could have her picture taken with the four faces in the background. Then again, maybe in her 'guy' clothes she didn't really want any pictures. This charade was less and less fun for her and she longed for a way out. What would Scott do if she showed up for work someday in shorts and a short-sleeved shirt? She wasn't brave enough to find out yet.

THE VIEW OF FIREWORKS exploding in the sky behind the faces on the mountain was spectacular. Everyone 'ooh'ed and 'aah'ed but Josie was so enthralled with the sight she couldn't say a word. After the show ended and they made their way down the mountain to the parking area the crowd was strangely subdued. A few tired children fussed, and you could hear parents encouraging them along with promises of a drink once they were at the car, or a candy bar, or whatever they had to bribe them with. But, otherwise, people just seemed intent on reaching their vehicles and getting home.

As they traveled back to Rapid City, Scott's family seemed all talked out so no one said much. Josie was enjoying the time for thought and retrospect. She was also feeling the need for a nice shower, a clean nightie, and her bed. The heavy clothing she'd had on most of the day had her feeling very dirty and sweaty. And most unfeminine.

Scott drove her to the shop yard where she'd left her pickup. Just as they pulled in, Scott asked her if she'd like to go to church Sunday.

"Church?"

"Yeah. You know, a minister, choir, song books, etc."

"Well, um, I guess, well, I don't have anything to wear. I only brought work clothes with me."

"Oh, no one worries about clothes. Some people come in jeans, some in shorts, some dress up a bit more but it's not a big deal," Scott assured her. "I think you'd like it. It's very friendly."

"Um, a, what church do you go to?"

"It's the Community Evangelical Church," Scott replied. "Pastor Art and Carolyn Johnson are a real nice middle-aged couple. They've been here a few years."

Josie's mind was frantically trying to figure a way out of this, but she was coming up blank. How could she refuse to go to church?

"Well, look, Josie. No pressure. I just thought you might like to go."

"I would like to go, Scott. I just don't know about the clothes deal," Josie lied. "Maybe another time, okay?"

"Sure. Fine. Well, see you on Monday then," Scott said.

"Uh, Scott, where is this church? Maybe I can figure out something to wear." Now why did I do that? I was off the hook and Scott didn't seem too upset with me. Why did I open my big mouth?

Scott left her with a smile and Josie drove to her rooming house regretting that she'd even gone to the 4th of July celebration. Now she was really in a bind.

Chapter 3

IN AN OUTFIT VERY similar to what she'd worn to the picnic, Josie showed up at the church at 10:30 Sunday morning. After she'd been handed a bulletin and shown to a seat, she looked around to see if there was anyone there that she knew. That was stupid. She was several hundred miles from home and knew no one in town except her boss and his family. She guessed that was just an automatic thing people did, look for familiar faces in a crowd.

Josie was thankful that the sanctuary was air-conditioned. It was already pretty hot outside when she drove over to the church. She'd been worried that she'd roast in these warm clothes. How nice it would be to put on a dress or even slacks and a lighter weight shirt. Why had she thought she could carry this 'guy' thing off? Had she ever even thought beyond the 'getting the job' aspect? She knew she could do the work so that hadn't ever been a part of her great plan. Now what? She couldn't go on like this forever.

An usher stood at the end of the pew she was sitting on and asked her to move further in so others could join her. A bit embarrassed that she hadn't thought to move in when she was seated, she stood quickly and walked to the other end of the pew and sat down. Until Scott sat down beside her she didn't realize that it was his family that was seated. He was grinning at her.

"What?" she snapped.

"Hey! I was just being friendly," he said, looking hurt.

"I'm sorry. Guess I got up on the wrong side of the bed this morning," Josie apologized. "Then I was feeling stupid for having to be told to move down."

"No problem. And it's not a big deal to be asked to move down. Happens to me nearly every service."

"Every service?"

"Pretty close. I guess I always think I can just have the whole pew to myself until they ask me to move. Kind of stupid, I guess."

"Well, it's nice to know I'm in good company." Josie grinned.

"Shhh!"

Scott turned to look at his parents and saw his mother with her finger on her lips. For evermore! He wasn't a child anymore! But she kept her finger in place until he nodded his agreement. He turned to Josie and said, "we have to be quiet now. It's time to start."

Josie was acutely aware of Scott sitting next to her. *This is crazy! He's just my boss!* But he was easy on the eyes. She thought back over the weeks she'd worked for him. *He was actually a very nice guy!* Suddenly Josie was aware that everyone was standing, and Scott shoved a songbook at her. She opened her mouth to try singing Amazing Grace, but she caught herself and nearly dropped the book. *Good gravy! I don't dare sing; that would be a dead give away.* So, she just looked at the book. Probably the only song they could have sung that she'd ever heard, and it almost tripped her up.

As the service progressed, Josie enjoyed the music, the preaching, and even the announcements. After the service everyone walked past the preacher and shook his hand on their way out. Scott introduced her to Pastor Art Johnson and explained that Josie worked for him. The preacher said he was glad to meet Josie and invited her back.

As Scott and Josie stood outside the church watching young couples come out with little children and babies, and older people holding on to each other, she felt something akin to loneliness sweep over her. *Will I ever be part of a family like that? Part of a friendly church congregation? Will I ever figure out where I belong?*

AFTER JOSIE HAD EATEN a light lunch she sat in her room and thought about the church service. Something the preacher said had really caught her attention. He'd said that no matter how good we all try to be, we all fall short of God's requirements. Because of that, no one can qualify to go to Heaven. He said that no matter how many good works we do, we have still sinned and are, thus, not allowed in Heaven.

Her mind had gotten so caught up in that thought and wondering how that could be fair that she'd missed the rest of what he said. Surely, God wouldn't just shut everyone out of Heaven? Even that preacher? Josie and her family had gone to church on special occasions, but she couldn't recall ever hearing anything about sin, or how you could get into Heaven. She'd just assumed that when you got there they checked to see if the good you did outweighed the bad and if it did, they let you in. But this guy sure didn't sound like he believed that. The Bible must tell something about it. Wonder if the rooming house is like a hotel and has a Bible in a drawer?

Josie knew she'd put clothing and other belongings in all of the drawers in the dresser in her room and she was sure she hadn't seen a Bible. But maybe there was something in the drawer in the little table the phone sat on. She looked but there was nothing there. Disappointed, she wandered around her room, feeling like there was something important she was missing out on but not knowing exactly what it was.

She picked up the bulletin she'd brought home from church and looked to see what kind of information was in it. The pastor's name was given, along with the youth minister and the minister of music. The church's phone number was also listed. But no home phone numbers were given. Then she noticed that the church had an evening service on Sunday as well as activities on Wednesday evenings. Maybe she could go to church tonight and get some answers?

Josie thought about going as herself, confident that no one from this morning would know the difference. But what if Scott was there? Would he be able to tell? In the end, it was too great a risk and she donned the same clothing she'd worn to the morning service. She slipped into a pew toward the back and waited for the service to begin. There was a Bible in a rack on the back of the pew in front of her and she picked it up. Flipping through the pages, she read a few lines here and there. Absolutely nothing made any sense to her. Maybe you had to go to college to learn how to understand it? Her dad had a Bible-she had seen it. In fact, all the births, deaths, and weddings from her parents and their parents and grandparents were written in it, somewhere. In the middle? Maybe in the back? She remembered seeing it once but couldn't remember what the occasion was. She'd never seen anyone looking at it or reading it, ever.

She realized that the service was beginning and resolved to pay close attention to everything they said. After they'd sung a couple of songs, taken an offering, and made some announcements, the preacher started preaching. He was talking about families and how parents were supposed to teach their children about God several times a day. She wondered if her parents had known. Must not. Surely, if they'd known they were supposed to do that, they would have done it. Her parents had taken parenting very seriously and had even taken classes at the local high school when she and her sister were little. Of course, after that her mom left and her dad was on his own.

Classes must not have made much of an impact on her mother. Or, maybe, they scared her away?

As she left after the service, the minister remembered her from the morning service. He said something very strange to her after he greeted her and thanked her for coming. "When you need to talk, call me or come on over."

WHEN she needed to talk? How did he know she would need to talk? And talk about what?

Josie's sleep was rather disturbed that night. She awoke to her alarm and with the feeling she'd had a very wild dream but with no memory of what it had been about. She didn't feel at all rested, nor did the idea of going to work hold much appeal. She got dressed, went down to the dining room to eat and then left for work but with absolutely none of the enthusiasm that had accompanied her every workday since she'd arrived.

Chapter 4

"Mornin' Josie," Scott greeted her. "You have a bad night?"

"Yeah. Didn't sleep much," she muttered. "What's up first?"

Scott handed her orders for a couple of minor repairs that he figured she could complete before lunch. She turned to go to her pickup, wanting to just get going, hoping she'd feel better as the day went on. "So, Josie, how'd you like church yesterday?"

"It was fine," Josie said, without slowing or looking back. She really wasn't in the mood for a discussion about anything, especially church. That's what kept her up last night. What's all this stuff about church being 'peaceful' or making you feel peace? Not that she could see! She'd probably had the least peaceful night's sleep she could ever remember. Not counting when she was little and her mother had left, of course.

Hmm. Scott wondered what had Josie's dander up. Grumpiest I've ever seen him. Maybe something struck a chord? So, this could be good! I might have to put up with a pretty grumpy worker while God works on him, but the end result will be worth it. I'll just step up my prayers. He smiled. Yeah, I'll step up my prayers, but I'll get a few more people praying, too. He reached for the phone to call his mom. After all, whatever else was wrong in this guy's life, everyone needed to know the peace of the Lord.

Josie's morning seemed to go from bad to worse. The first job was to replace the second step on Mrs. Brownell's front porch. Should have been an easy, relatively quick job. Just take the old step off, cut the wood the right length and nail in the new step. The customer was even going to paint it herself. What could go wrong? Right! What couldn't go wrong?

First, the neighbor's dog had bitten Josie's leg, enough to draw blood. She'd had to go to the emergency care center for a tetanus shot. That was just downright aggravating. Of course, they'd also cleaned and bandaged her wound and suggested a mild pain medication. Josie didn't want to take anything for pain; what was she, a wimp? But the leg sort of throbbed all morning.

Back on the job, Josie proceeded to pry the old board up. It had split and flown into her face where the nail grazed her cheek. She'd watched her tongue but inside she'd said some less than ladylike phrases. Once she had the old board off, she'd measured the old board twice, just to be sure, and then measured and cut the plank she had brought. Right where she needed to saw the wood, there'd been a rather nasty knothole, so she'd flipped the board and measured from the other end. That seemed to go okay but as she laid the saw down, she'd managed to drop it on her left hand. That hurt.

When she finally left the job all she really wanted to do was go home, take a nice long shower and go to bed. But she turned the pickup toward Fifth Street and her second job of the morning. This one was to replace several pickets in the fence that ran alongside the owner's property. This customer wanted Josie to paint the pickets, but she had her own paint. Josie got the boards cut to the right size and sprayed them with a first coat of paint. While they dried, she replaced the horizontal boards in the fence and sprayed them as well. It was a quick drying first coat that she always carried. Once the fence was completed, Josie would return to brush paint it but using this first coat always seemed to speed things up and make the second coat cover better.

When she had the fencing completed, she promised the customer she'd return later in the afternoon and paint the fence and then turned her pickup toward the shop. On the way she stopped for a burger and some fries and swung by her rooming house for some aspirin. By now she was wishing she'd accepted whatever the Dr. had offered for the pain.

Scott heard Josie's truck pull into the shop yard and grinned. Wonder if he's in any better humor, he wondered. When he heard the pickup door slam shut he shook his head. Apparently not. Wonder exactly what got under Josie's skin? I don't remember anything from the sermon that would have riled anyone up. On the other hand, I have no way of knowing how the words sounded to someone coming from a different perspective. Is it safe to ask, he wondered?

Josie stomped into the shop with the work tickets in one hand and her lunch in the other. Stopping at the pop machine, she bought a coke and downed the aspirin and then set her lunch down on a workbench. She handed Scott the ticket from Mrs. Brownell's and explained that she'd have to go back to the second job a little later in the afternoon. "Shouldn't take more than 30 minutes to paint that fence," she assured Scott.

"So, everything go okay?" Scott inquired. When Josie's face clouded over, he thought better of asking the question. This might be a good time to shut up and eat. If Josie didn't answer, Scott decided he'd wait until after they'd eaten and rested up a bit before asking again.

"First job was not my best day," Josie grumbled. "Neighbor's dog bit me. I had to go get a tetanus shot. Then the board split and hit me in the face." She pulled her hair back just enough for Scott to see the red trail the nail had left on her cheek.

"Wow! Man, I'm sorry you had such a lousy morning." Scott thought that Josie actually seemed to be handling it fairly well. He wasn't too much grumpier than he'd been when he left the shop at 8:00. "Neighbor have insurance for the shot?"

"Yeah. She actually drove me there, fussing all the way. If my shots had been current, I wouldn't have bothered. But I don't think I've had one for several years and couldn't see having to pay for it myself when it was her dog that caused the problem." Josie almost smiled. "Stupid little mutt. Why is it that it's always the little ones that bite?"

Scott laughed. "I know. I couldn't tell you how many big dogs have barked and scared me spitless but now I only worry about the little ones. They're sneaky, too." Josie nodded. Scott continued, "So, how much damage did the mutt inflict?"

Josie started to roll her pants leg up to show him and then remembered that her shapely, shaved leg might not be quite what Scott was expecting to see. "Oh, it's too high. It broke the skin enough to bleed," and she pointed to her pant leg. "It really didn't look that bad but it sure is painful."

"You want to knock off for the day?"

"Naw. Might as well work. It'll probably be sore for a couple days no matter what I'm doing. Besides, I have to go back and paint that fence."

"If you're sure?"

"Yeah. What else do you have for this afternoon, anyway?"

Scott briefed Josie on a couple smaller jobs, and they discussed the best way to go about replacing the bedroom window that Mrs. Clanton wanted done. She'd bought the window from a local discount store, but Scott didn't know if she'd gotten the right thing or not. They decided that Josie would double-check that before she did anything else. They didn't want the window out, ready for the new one, and then find out that the new one wasn't going to work for some reason.

They'd sort of lapsed into a companionable silence and Scott thought Josie looked like it wouldn't take much to fall asleep. He said a quiet prayer and then tried to ease into a conversation about church yesterday. Josie didn't show any willingness to talk about it, so Scott figured he'd better to just drop it for now.

The phone rang. Scott chatted and laughed for a couple of minutes and then turned back to tell Josie the joke. Josie was not there and when Scott looked outside, the pickup was gone. Guess he really didn't want to talk about it.

Just keep praying, Scott, he told himself. Just keep praying.

TUESDAY MORNING JOSIE SEEMED in better humor. At least the door slamming didn't jar the windows in the shop. Scott wondered if he'd slept better. That was the only reason Josie had given for his lousy humor the day before.

"Hey, Josie! You don't look quite so fierce this morning. Safe to talk to you today?"

Josie looked a bit embarrassed. "Sorry. I don't usually get like that. Don't know why I couldn't sleep Sunday night. Too much on my mind, I guess."

"Well, it's getting pretty hot out. You got air conditioning or a fan in that room of yours?"

"No. It was kind of hot. Mrs. Stewart said she had some fans and she'd get them out."

"She's waited this long? Why, it's July! What's she thinking?"

Josie grinned. "Yeah. She said that the nights have been cooling down so well she didn't think we'd need the fans. But since Sunday night was so hot she decided she'd better get them out."

"She cheap about everything?" Scott asked. "Like, how good is the food you get there?"

"She's not going to break the bank buying groceries but it's not too bad."

"I don't know why I didn't think of it sooner, but my mom's door is always open. She fusses about me like she never taught me to cook a thing. I'm always welcome at dinnertime, she says, and then adds that I can bring friends any time. We should wander over there at least once a week. She's really a good cook."

"That doesn't sound bad," Josie agreed. "But I wouldn't want to wear out my welcome."

Scott related stories about showing up at his folks' with six or seven other guys in tow. "Never even phased her. I don't know how she did it, but we never ran out of food."

"My dad was kind of like that, too," Josie added. "I never pushed it that far, though. But once my sister brought home her whole cheerleading squad and I thought my dad was going to have a fit. But he handled it pretty well." Josie grinned. "But he made a point of telling us both that if we wanted to bring more than two we should give him fair warning."

"Seems only fair," Scott chuckled. "Parents are pretty amazing!"

AFTER THEY'D REVIEWED THE tickets for Monday and Scott had clarified a couple of questions Josie had about the billing, they went over the tickets for today. As Josie left for her first job, Scott had a thought.

"Josie? You play any sports?"

"Now?"

"Or ever?"

"Not really. Played some soccer in grade school. But once I started working with my dad, there just never seemed to be time for sports."

"Hey! Soccer is my sport of choice; I've played since I was a kid. But now I also play on the church softball team. Games are on Friday night. Wanna come and hang out? Or join us?"

"Never played baseball," Josie said. "I could come cheer you on, I guess. It's not like I'm too busy."

"Any time!" Scott grinned. "Nice bunch of guys. Plus, a lot of the gals come to watch. Never know who you might meet."

"Any special girls for you, Scott?"

"Why, Josie. I thought you knew; they're all special."

Josie shook her head and grabbed her tool belt. "Later."

IN HER PICKUP, HEADED for Canyon Lake Drive, Josie thought about the soccer. She'd really enjoyed it and hadn't been a bad player. Once she quit to work, it just never seemed like she could get back in it. She wondered if Scott was a good player. Hmm. Wonder if they play indoors here in the winter? She'd have to ask. They couldn't play softball in the winter, could they? Of course, she'd have to come clean about who she was before she could play soccer or anything else. Somehow baggy pants and long-sleeved shirts didn't quite sound apropos for an indoor soccer game.

IN THE SHOP SCOTT was humming to himself, rather pleased that his invitation to come to softball had seemed to go over okay. Maybe he'd found a key to Josie. I don't know what it is about him but there's something missing or wrong or whatever. But I know one thing. Everyone needs to know Jesus, regardless of what their problems are.

That's the most he's talked about his family. Wonder if that's part of the problem? If he liked working for his dad so much, why did he pull up stakes and move to Rapid City? He'd never said anything to indicate that his relationship with his dad had any problems. Maybe there'd been a girl?

Scott called his mom to see if any one night this week would be better than another for bringing Josie over. Now that he'd bragged about her he wanted to make sure the invitation was still open. They talked about his concern for Josie's spiritual needs and prayed together before Scott got back to work. Any night, she'd said, would be fine. Scott laughed quietly. Maybe we can just win him with kindness. Sure can't hurt.

JOSIE WAS GRATEFUL THAT this morning was going much better than yesterday. She'd always joked with her dad about the 'Monday morning blues' and they'd tried to figure out why Mondays were so often difficult.

Her dad blamed it on church. Said all those 'Christians' forgot about the real world over the weekend, so it was a real shock on Monday. Knowing Scott, Josie was beginning to doubt her dad's opinion. At least, since she'd been to church with him and his family, she assumed they were Christians. That probably explained a lot about Scott. She'd never seen him lose his temper or heard him swear or even talk about someone in an unkind way. And he sure wasn't grumpy on Monday! Maybe too cheerful, sometimes, she thought. He doesn't seem to get rattled about much.

Wonder what it is that lets him seem so peaceful? Not worried? She assumed he earned enough with the shop to take care of his needs, but he didn't drive a new, fancy truck or anything. What kind of place does he live in? Josie pulled up the address on the work ticket. Another fence to patch. She buckled on her tool belt as she walked to the door. Time to get to work.

Chapter 5

FRIDAY AS THEY WERE leaving the shop Scott asked Josie if she'd like to come to his softball game.

"You need a cheering section, do you?" Josie half smiled. "I guess if you're that hard up I could come by for a while. Where do you play?"

Scott gave her directions to the Star of the West sports complex. "There are softball fields kind of toward the middle and soccer fields around three sides. Works out pretty good most of the time."

Josie nodded. "I think I drove by there one day when I was out wandering. I'll see you about seven?"

"Yup. That'd just about do it." Scott seemed pleased she would come. I'll have to be careful not to start really sounding like a cheerleader. Might be a bit suspicious. The fact that she knew next to nothing about baseball could save her from herself. Be a little hard to cheer intelligently when she had no idea what was going on. Her dad had hated baseball, so they'd never watched it on television and certainly neither she nor Hope had played the game. Guess it could be interesting.

I'll see what's for dinner at the rooming house. If it isn't to my liking, I might pick up something on my way to the game. Sure would be nice to shower and change into something a bit more comfortable in this heat. Like shorts and a tee shirt. Or at least a short-sleeved shirt. Nope. Can't do that. My own fault. This lie is beginning to take on a life of its own and I don't like it one bit. But how to get out of it?

SCOTT PULLED INTO THE parking lot at the fields and looked around for Josie's truck. Not here yet. It'll be nice to have him here to cheer us on. Maybe I can talk him into joining us one of these days if I'm patient. Josie doesn't seem to want to commit to much, I've noticed. Seems kind of lost.

They were in the bottom of the first inning when Scott looked toward the bleachers and saw Josie sitting there munching on something. Must not have had anything he liked at his rooming house. Again. Too bad he didn't have kitchen privileges. At least then he could make something he liked. Of course, that would only be possible if he knew how to cook. Scott grinned. Josie seemed to know how to do most anything. Kind of a handy man to have around. He chuckled at his own joke. Handy man.

As the game progressed, Scott was trying to focus on the game. The other team was very good and had beaten them every time they'd played last summer and so far, this year. By the end of the seventh inning they were tied at 4 runs each and Scott's team was playing like they were all out of gas. Getting too old for this game? Naw. Not at 28! Guess we need to start running or something to build up some endurance. 'Course it wouldn't hurt if we did more during the winter so we could come into the softball season in better shape. Maybe we should see about playing some indoor soccer during the winter. That would be fun! Maybe Josie would join us.

Oops! We're up. I've missed the last play with my mind wandering. Better be paying better attention. He glanced at the scoreboard. Nope. No change. He took up his position at 3rd base and scanned the dugout to see the batting order for the other team. Two really strong hitters right off the bat. This could be a long inning.

JOSIE WATCHED THE GAME with little interest. Not her sport. She knew the basics but not the finer points, so she wasn't always sure what the calls meant. At least it was almost over and she could head for home and the shower. As she watched, the batter hit the ball almost straight up into the air. The pitcher ran forward a few steps and caught it. Hmm. That should make that batter out? Yup. He went back to the dugout and another player took his place to bat.

Josie's mind wandered to her dad. How was he doing without her on the job? They'd worked together so well for so long that it still seemed strange not to be working with him. But she'd gotten to the point where she felt she had to strike out on her own. She needed to make it without his good name. By herself. Where no one would hire her because of him or refuse to hire her because of him or refuse to hire her because she was female. She needed to do it now, not wait until her dad was gone and find herself unemployable. So, she'd left. He understood. At least he said he did, but she knew he was still a little hurt about it. That's why she called every week so they could stay tight. Her mom had left them all when Josie was only seven. In learning to get along without her, they'd all gotten very close. Her sister, Hope, had learned to cook, although they all helped. Still, Hope did more of the homey things and Josie tended toward the outdoor stuff like the yard work or helping her dad on projects. It had worked pretty well for the three of them and they gradually stopped talking about their mom. They'd heard from her on birthdays and Christmas the first few years and then nothing. Josie was 24 now and the last time she'd gotten a card from her mom had been on her tenth birthday.

Suddenly Scott was poking her in the arm. "So, whadja think? They're a pretty good team and this is the first time in two summers we've beaten them!"

"Great!" Josie started to jump to her feet, but Scott sat down.

"Naw. Let's sit a bit. I need to cool down." Scott was all smiles.

"Did you enjoy the game?"

"Sure. It was great," Josie lied. "I'm not much of a baseball fan so I don't understand all the calls and stuff."

"It's not baseball. It's softball," Scott corrected her. "But it doesn't matter. They're similar. Glad you came. Nice to look over and see someone on our side."

"Didn't seem like either team had too many fans," Josie observed. "More of a participation sport than a spectator sport?"

"Yeah. I guess in a way most sports are. It's much more fun to play than watch," Scott agreed. "I can get pretty caught up in a soccer game if it's World Cup or something like that. Otherwise, I'd rather be playing."

Josie nodded her head in agreement. "When I played soccer in grade school, I knew a girl who would watch taped world cup games all the time. She'd stop the tape whenever she saw a move she liked, back it up, watch it in slow motion, back it up, watch it again and finally, if she needed to, she'd do it frame by frame. Then she'd go out and work on that move until she had it down pat. She really got to be a great player."

"You played with girls?" Scott asked.

"We had mixed teams. More boys than girls. Later, as we got older and the sport caught on more, we went to separate teams. But the girls who had played on the boys' teams were much stronger players than the girls who waited to play until they had all girl and all boy teams."

"What about the boys?"

"What do you mean?"

"Did playing on mixed teams affect the quality of play for the boys?"

'Maybe. I guess I don't really know. I quit playing when I was in the 8th grade because by then I was going with my dad several days a week after school and always on weekends. I didn't keep track too much. My sister, Hope, played through high school so she talked about the girl's teams. The only time she ever talked about the boy's teams was when she had a crush on one of the goalies." Josie grinned. "That was really something!"

"Why?" Scott couldn't help but ask.

"Hope's a pretty good player but when this one guy was around, she almost couldn't walk and chew gum at the same time. He showed up at a game once and Hope was done for. Couldn't complete a pass, couldn't do a throw in, couldn't find another player on her team, couldn't. . . well, she couldn't do anything! It was amazing! She was humiliated and didn't want to go to school the next day. Dad refused to let her skip and she was really mad at him. I found out later that she'd forged a note from Dad excusing her and got away with it. I don't think Dad ever found out."

"Aha! Blackmail material for you, huh?" Scott teased. "Bet you used it, too!"

"Naw. Well, I did use it one time."

Suddenly Josie stood up, picked up her trash and started toward the parking lot. "See ya Monday, Scott. Thanks for the invite!"

"But aren't you going to tell me. . .hey, Josie! What's the hurry?"

Scott ran to catch up to Josie. "Hey, man. Wait up."

Josie slowed down and turned. "What's up? Thought we were leaving?"

"So I see. I thought we were still talking," Scott puffed. "Give me a break, I just played a game and I'm out of wind."

"Out of condition is more like it," Josie retorted. "Just how old are you, anyway?"

"Probably about the same as you. I'm 28."

"Yup! Old age has crept in. You poor old thing!" Josie was enjoying this. Scott really was having trouble keeping up and talking at the same time. "Course, it IS Friday, so you've worked hard all week. Probably used up your quota of energy and now you're out til what, Monday? When do you get your new allotment?"

"You know, for someone I thought was rather quiet a few weeks ago, you've got a real nasty streak in you, Josie!" Scott was trying to look hurt but Josie couldn't help but laugh.

"Hey! You actually laughed!" Scott teased. "I thought that was against your religion!"

"Me!? I got no religion!" Josie stated flatly. "Don't think God much likes me." Then before Scott could reply, Josie turned toward her pickup and waved to Scott. "See ya Monday, boss man!"

"Hey, wait. I wondered if you wanted to meet up at church again on Sunday?"

"Well, like I said, God don't like me much. Not sure he'd appreciate me darkening his doors another Sunday."

"Oh, you got that all wrong. He loves you, just like He loves me, and He'd love to see you at church," Scott replied.

"Yeah. Right. I'll think on it. At 10:30? If I decide to come?"

Scott agreed and Josie swung up into her truck, started the engine, and started backing up. Slowly, so Scott would move out of her way. That guy just didn't give up!

God loved her! Yeah, right. So much that the Bible she'd read at church last Sunday said He wouldn't let anyone into His heaven. That was love, all right! What about Scott and his family and that minister? It didn't make sense that they'd keep going to church and being good people if they couldn't ever get into heaven. If that's love, she thought, maybe I don't need it.

RELUCTANTLY DONNING HER USUAL wardrobe, Josie made her way to church. This time she took a seat near the back and buried herself in the bulletin, hoping no one would notice her. Glancing up from time to time she saw Scott sit down about a third of the way back. Later she saw that his family had joined him. He was looking around, probably trying to see if she was there but she kept her head down and he didn't see her. She hoped.

The service began and Josie braced herself. For what she wasn't certain. The singing, announcements and offering passed with no problems for her. Then the pastor began to preach. Josie was determined to follow him closely to find out why he was preaching about a God and Heaven that seemed unattainable to her. There had to be more to this than she'd grasped so far.

Again, he said that God would allow no one with sin in their life to enter Heaven. No one could ever earn Heaven, purchase entrance, or do enough good deeds to get in. So, he said, God sent his son, Jesus, to pay the price for everyone to get in. Okay! Now we're getting somewhere! There IS a way in. Oops. Lost him again. If Jesus paid for everyone to get in then apparently everyone really was going to Heaven! No, wait. The pastor was saying that a person had to accept Jesus and his sacrifice in order to become His child and enter Heaven. So, what's the problem? Who wouldn't accept that kind of deal?

On her way out she asked Pastor Johnson if he had any time for her. He said they could talk for a while after everyone left if she would like to hang around a while. Otherwise, they could set something else up. Josie opted to stay and went back inside the sanctuary to wait for the pastor.

Pastor Johnson explained salvation through Jesus and Josie prayed with him. "Now, Josie, you need to start reading the Bible to learn more about Jesus and how He wants us to live."

"The Bible! I tried that a couple of Sundays ago and couldn't understand anything I read."

"Read the gospel of John, Josie. When you're through, read it again. If you have any questions, be sure to call me. I'm starting a class on Tuesday evenings for new Christians. Would you like to join us?"

Josie left church with a new Bible, courtesy of the church, and a bookmarker with the pastor's phone number and the date and time for the new class. Her heart felt a little lighter and she wore a smile as she climbed into her truck and headed for home. So, God did really love her after all!

SCOTT WAS HAVING DINNER with his family. Mom's cooking was definitely better than his and he enjoyed the banter with his siblings.

Not that he couldn't cook pretty well if he wanted to, it was just too much of a bother just for himself. He found he ate a lot of fried egg sandwiches and soup if he wasn't careful.

"I didn't see your friend Josie at church this morning, did I?" his dad asked. "Course, I wasn't really looking that hard."

"Nope, I didn't see him either. He came to our softball game Friday night and I asked him, but he didn't commit either way. I don't think he's comfortable in church. I get the feeling it's not a place he's been to very often."

"All the more reason for him to come," Barb added. "But, of course, you can't shove it down his throat either."

"Yup," Scott agreed and took his sister's hand as they all joined hands to pray. "Amen. This really looks good, Mom."

Barb Mayforth smiled fondly at her oldest child. He would eat her out of house and home if he still lived with them. "Glad you like it, Scottie."

"Yeah, Scottie," his sister piped up. "It's just been so long since you ate with us. What is it, one day? You *were* here yesterday for lunch, weren't you?

"Yeah, yeah, Cindy," Scott responded. "I have to come around pretty often to keep you in line."

Cindy had a mouthful so just lightly hit him in the arm. As she swallowed, she turned to him. "Like you could!"

Scott was too busy eating to respond so he just ignored her. She had been a pest for as long as he could remember. Well, not really. He remembered when she was born, he was eleven, but sometimes it sure seemed like forever. He wouldn't trade her but he'd never tell her that. Remembering how he and Terry had ganged up on her through the years brought a smile to his face.

"What?" Cindy demanded.

"Just remembering how Terry and I pushed you off the diving board at the pool that summer. You scared us both to death, acting like you got hurt and were drowning," Scott growled.

"Served you both right," Cindy retorted. "I thought I did pretty good."

Terry added, "You sure scared me, that's for sure."

Cindy just grinned. She'd figured out how to deal with both of them at a pretty young age. Self defense.

As the Mayforth family finished eating, Scott helped Barb clear the table and load the dishwasher. That was always the best opportunity to talk to his mom and he enjoyed it. Jim and Terry made their way to the living room and started through the Sunday paper. Cindy fixed herself a glass of iced tea and took a book into the back yard to enjoy under the big oak tree.

"Say, Mom," Scott began. "do you think there's anything kind of different about Josie?"

"Different, how?"

"I don't know. There's something about him that just doesn't ring true but I have no idea what it is. He's a good worker. Pretty strong for such a little guy. He talks a little bit about his family but not a lot. Seems to have a good sense of humor and gets along with the customers well. I just don't know."

"Well, we don't know what his life was like or what his family is like, Scott. There may have been problems there. He does seem like a nice young man and we have enjoyed having him with us."

"Yeah. Guess I'm just imagining things again." Scott dried the roaster pan his mother had just washed. As he put it away their conversation turned to other things. After thanking his mom for dinner, Scott waved to the rest of the family and headed for his own place. He had done his laundry yesterday and straightened up so he figured he'd better get his bookwork done for the week. He felt a bit guilty, as he knew he shouldn't be working on the Lord's day. But it only took him an hour or so and he just couldn't ever seem to get it done on Saturday.

Chapter 6

SCOTT HEARD JOSIE'S TRUCK pull into the work yard and smiled. This guy made him smile sometimes and he didn't know why. It wasn't that Josie was funny and made him laugh, not real often, anyway. Just smile. Hmm?

Josie came in with her usual, "Good morning, boss. Ready to work?"

Scott smiled again.

"What?" Josie demanded. "What's so funny?"

"Nothing. I just like to smile sometimes. Keeps my face in practice."

Josie just shook her head. "You're nuts!"

"Maybe. Hey, my mom wondered why you weren't in church yesterday."

"What? I go once and now I'm on report if I don't show up?"

"No. I didn't mean that. Just thought you'd like to know that she was looking for you. I think she likes you."

"Oh. Okay. What's up first?"

"Anxious to get to work, huh? You'd think I was a slave driver."

Scott grinned. "I was going to send you over to repair or replace a door, whichever is the best. But I just got another call. I kind of know these people, they've lived around here for a long time and I've done work for them from time to time. But Mrs. Russell said she thinks he's getting Alzheimer's and she's pretty upset. He was going to replace one of their steps, but he cut the wood wrong. She said he was really frustrated but she encouraged him to try again. Finally, she said he came in the house quite angry. Kept saying, 'I've cut it three times and it's still too short. What am I going to do?'

"Oh, man. That don't sound good."

"No. I don't think it is. She had to call the Dr. and they sent an ambulance to take him to the hospital. They're keeping him for observation, she said. A couple days, at least."

"Wow. That's really sad."

"Yeah. Anyway, I'd like you to go take care of this for her first thing. At least she won't have to worry about the step."

"Yeah," Josie responded, "and then neither of them can trip on it or something. Sounds like they don't need any more trouble."

Josie loaded some supplies and headed for the address on Jackson Blvd. She'd started the morning feeling pretty good, even thought about telling Scott that she'd prayed with the pastor. But this was so sad. Just thinking that something like that could happen to her dad nearly made her cry. Then she thought about telling him that she was going to church and could almost hear his response. Maybe she wasn't quite ready for that conversation.

Pulling up to the address she parked the truck and went to the door. A little old lady who looked about eighty answered her knock. She looked so lost that Josie had to stop herself from just putting her arms around her and telling her that it would be okay. Knowing she needed to be professional she took a deep breath. "Good morning, Mrs. Russell?"

"Yes. Are you the young man that Scott sent?"

"Yes, ma'am. I'll get right to work on that step for you. I'm guessing it's on the back of the house?"

"Yes. You can just come on through and I'll show you."

"Oh, Mrs. Russell. I'd rather walk around and meet you there if that's okay. I hate the idea of getting any dirt on your floor."

The little old lady hesitated, then smiled. "That's very considerate of you, young man. I'll meet you there."

Happy that she'd gotten a smile out of Mrs. Russell, Josie walked around to the back door of the house. She assured Mrs. Russell that she'd get right on it and pulled out her tape to get the measurements she'd need.

When she had the step in place, she knocked on the door to see if Mrs. Russell wanted her to paint the step. She was taken to the garage and shown the paint to be used. She carried brushes and the like with her, so she got busy and painted the step. Letting Mrs. Russell know she was finished she returned to the shop.

"I didn't know if you wanted me to give her a ticket and collect or not so just told her good-bye and left," she reported to Scott.

"That's best. Thanks, Josie. How'd Mrs. Russell seem to you?" he asked.

They talked about the Russells and their problems for a couple of minutes then Scott gave Josie the work ticket for the door job he'd mentioned earlier.

The rest of the day and the next went by rather quickly and soon it was Tuesday night. Josie was at the church a few minutes early and sat in her truck. She had the Bible the pastor had given her, but she'd only gotten a few chapters in John read so she read another while waiting for other cars to show up. Jesus really seemed like a nice guy. Was He really the Son of God? Wow. Why would He want to leave a nice place like Heaven and come live down here?

When she saw the pastor arrive and unlock the door she got out of her truck. She'd brought a notebook along and grabbed that and her Bible and went inside, hoping she wouldn't be asked questions she couldn't answer.

But the pastor, whom everyone seemed to be calling 'PJ' welcomed her and a few others and they all sat down, some a bit warily, and he opened with a simple prayer. That didn't seem too scary, so Josie relaxed a bit.

Everyone introduced themselves and said what they did, where they lived and how long they'd been Christians. Josie seemed to be the newest and everyone congratulated her and shook her hand. The pastor said, "I'd like to keep this real informal. We'll go slow and answer any questions anyone may have as we go. You all can call me either Pastor Johnson or just PJ."

A teenage girl questioned the 'PJ' nickname. "It started out as 'Pastor Junior' because my dad was the minister and most of the congregation just called him Pastor. When I finished Seminary, I served as the junior pastor for a couple of years. Eventually they shortened it to PJ. It just stuck," he said, grinning, "and I got used to it."

Josie seemed to have more questions than any of the others, but everyone encouraged her to speak up and they all brought their own experiences and questions to the discussion. After an hour or so, PJ called a break and invited them to enjoy coffee, cookies, pop, etc. Then they went back to the Bible for another 30 to 40 minutes. Then PJ asked them to all join hands, and they went around the circle with each person praying a short prayer if they wanted to. Josie just listened and no one commented that she hadn't prayed. PJ closed them with a blessing, and they all headed toward the parking lot.

As Josie reached her pickup, one of the young couples called to her.

"We were wondering if you'd like to come over for dinner after church on Sunday?"

"Me?"

They laughed. "Yes, you. If you'd rather not, it's okay. But if you'd like to come we'd love to have you."

"That would be really nice. But you don't have to do that."

"We'd really love to get to know you better."

Josie thanked them and they agreed she'd follow them home after church Sunday. They waved and she drove off. Wow. Imagine that! I only met them tonight and I'm invited to dinner. Uh-oh! They probably figure I'm a poor guy who couldn't cook so they befriended me. But what would they think if they knew I'm a gal? Maybe I shouldn't go.

As she set her things out for work tomorrow and readied herself for bed, she wondered what Scott would think? I'm going to have to find a way to tell him. It's just too hard to keep up the pretense. Besides, I'm starting to like him. Really like him. He'll have to see me as a female before I'll know if I have any kind of chance with him. Her last thought was that she'd tell him tomorrow.

Scott was at the shop early on Wednesday morning. He needed to finish the cabinet he was building for the Mantheys. They'd called him at home the night before and really needed to get the cabinet in quickly, if possible, as they'd just learned they had company coming in just a week or so. Scott had promised he'd try to get it finished by Wednesday evening.

As he sanded the surface of the top drawer his mind drifted to Josie. Wonder if he'd like to go down to Custer State Park and attend the Playhouse? Scott and his brother had talked about going down in the next week or two when they found out what was playing. Terry wouldn't mind if they included Josie. Maybe he'd ask him when he came in.

Scott hummed as he worked. He loved the feel of the wood and the satiny finish he'd applied. Someday he'd build himself a house and make all of his cabinets. He'd gradually accumulated enough different saws and routers that he could do a large variety of trims and designs. The more he did the more he wanted to do. Wonder if I could just build cabinets and make a living at it? Maybe someday.

When the door opened, and Josie breezed in Scott jumped. "Wow! Is it that time already? I didn't know it was getting so late."

"Late? I'm not late!" Josie protested. "It's not even eight yet."

"No. I didn't mean you were late," Scott explained. "I came in early to work on this and the time went by so fast it startled me when you came in.

"That the one you're doing for those folks over off Canyon Lake Drive?"

"Yup. What do you think?"

"I'd take it in a heartbeat. I'm sure they'll be happy with it," Josie replied. "You really dig doing that stuff, don't you?"

"Does it show?" Scott grinned. "I thought I was doing a better job of hiding my enjoyment. Want it to seem like work so you'll feel sorry for me when I have to work late or come in early."

"Fat chance!" Josie stuck her sack lunch in the refrigerator. Taking a deep breath, she turned toward Scott. "I have something to tell you."

"You have what?"

"Something to tell.." The ringing of the phone interrupted, and Josie felt herself breathe out. She hadn't realized she was holding her breath.

Maybe this wasn't a good time to talk to Scott about this. Maybe tomorrow would be better.

Scott was still talking to his caller, so Josie took the clipboard and looked at the top couple of work tickets. Scott usually had them in the order he wanted them done in, so it was probably pretty safe to head on out to the jobs and talk to Scott later. She held the clipboard up so Scott would look at her and pointed to the door. He nodded his head, so she grabbed the supplies she'd need and left.

When she came back in just before lunchtime Scott had an emergency job that she needed to get to. She grabbed her lunch from the fridge, took the ticket from Scott and turned her truck toward Lemmon Ave in the north part of the town. Sounded like another flood like she'd encountered on her first day. Glad she'd brought her lunch she munched on a sandwich as she drove.

The problem on Lemmon Ave. turned out to be a busted pipe under the sink. Once Josie got the water turned off she stepped back so the lady could mop up the kitchen floor. Lady said her name was Margie and that she sure appreciated Josie getting there so quickly. While Margie got the worst of the water soaked up Josie went to her truck for the supplies she needed. Good thing she carried some pipes, fittings and sealant.

The job didn't really take too long but Josie had a hard time getting away from Margie. Such a pleasant lady but she really did like to visit. She was just so grateful that the problem was fixed that she kept thanking Josie over and over again. Josie finally wrote out a ticket and collected the money and was on her way.

She chuckled as she drove back to the shop. That Margie had been so nice and it was great to feel she'd really helped her. But that little lady could win, hands down, any talking contest she might ever enter.

WHEN SHE GOT BACK to the shop, Scott was talking on the phone. He held up his hand to acknowledge Josie as she entered. Then he motioned her over and said, "Hey Josie, I'm talking to my brother Terry that you met the 4th. He and I want to go to a production of the Playhouse down in Custer State Park either next weekend or the weekend after. We wondered if you'd like to tag along?"

"Just you two?" Josie asked. Scott nodded his head and Josie said she'd like to go if it worked out okay.

The rest of the week flew by and Scott asked Josie if she was coming to the softball game that night. "Maybe you'd like to join the team? We could use an extra body," he invited.

"I know nothing about that game and I sure don't belong on no team" Josie groused.

"Okay, okay! So you don't want to play. Want to come watch? We're going for pizza after."

"Naw. I don't know any of those guys. I wouldn't be comfortable going for pizza with your team. I might come by and watch a bit."

"Okay. See ya later, then."

Josie started out the door but stopped when Scott said, "Hey, the other day you said you had something to tell me?"

"It'll keep," Josie almost ran to her truck, jumped in and headed out.

'I don't think I'm quite ready for this conversation,' she thought. Not ready at all.

Chapter 7

THE WEEKEND PASSED ABOUT the same as the ones before it; Josie watched part of Scott's softball game on Friday night, did her laundry on Saturday, called her dad that evening, went to church on Sunday morning. The big change was that she paid a different kind of attention in church; she was much more interested in the words of the songs and the minister's sermon. She had so much to learn. Even the words of the songs they sang sometimes helped her understand something better.

This time she sat with Scott and his family, at their invitation. As everyone stood around outside talking after the service Terry reminded Josie that they would attend the Playhouse soon and said he was looking forward to it. Josie agreed. She'd never been to Custer State Park so was looking forward to that, also.

"If we go on a Saturday night, we could leave a few hours early and spend some time in the Park before the play," Terry agreed. "It'll be fun. I never get tired of seeing all the buffalo along with the other critters that live there. And, other than the year so much of the Park burned, it's always beautiful down there."

"Why did the Park burn?" Josie asked.

"It was a real dry year here and lightning started the fire and they just couldn't get it out until it had burned a lot of timber. Not a pretty sight." He shuddered.

"Was it long enough ago that the Park has pretty much recovered now?"

"It's in pretty good shape. Here in the Black Hills we are always aware of the dryness and fire danger during the summer. It's not so bad the years we get lots of snow in the winter and then have a wet spring. But the dry years keep everyone a bit nervous," Terry explained.

"It seems there have been a lot of bad fires across the country these past several years," Josie commented.

Scott had walked up and added his opinion to the discussion which very quickly included Jim and Barb as well. It seemed that Terry wasn't exaggerating about everyone being conscious of the fire danger in the Hills and everyone had a tidbit or two to contribute. Josie felt she learned more in that short conversation than she had in a semester of school.

"Josie, dear, would you like to join us for dinner?" Barb asked. "If you have no plans, we'd love to have you."

Jim said, "Sure, come on over. We always have plenty and Barb's an excellent cook." He patted his tummy and grinned. "Of course, sometimes her cooking's a bit too good."

Josie smiled and thanked them for the invitation but explained that she was invited to dinner elsewhere today.

"Oh. Well, that's very nice, dear, and I'm sure you'll have a great time." Barb looked sincerely disappointed and Josie thought Scott also looked unhappy with her answer.

Smiling, Josie said she'd love to come another time if they'd have her. Barb immediately invited her for the next Sunday and Josie accepted.

Grateful for their friendship and kindness, Josie excused herself and went to find the young couple who had invited her. Tim and Connie Adamson were waiting near their vehicle, so Josie followed them home. They lived off Sheridan Lake road, so Josie saw another part of this spread out town. They told her that she should remember to drive out their way in December as many people decorated their homes and yards with many, many lights.

"It's beautiful," Connie said, smiling. "If you like Christmas lights, this is the road to check out."

She had prepared a simple meal of salads, sandwiches and fruit. "We don't like a lot of hot food during the summer," she explained. "We don't have air conditioning, so I try not to heat up the house too much by cooking."

"This is wonderful!" Josie assured her. "I don't usually like to eat the heavier foods in the summertime, either. Seems like you just don't feel as good as you do if you eat light."

"We kind of learned this over the past four or five years," Tim added. "It took us a while to figure out what we liked the best during the hot months."

"My sister tried to get away with this with my dad, but he grew up eating big meals all year round and just didn't think he'd been fed if we had a lighter meal." Josie laughed. "He kind of likes things to stay the same."

Tim agreed. "My dad's the same way. Just doesn't like things to change."

"I think we're all that way to a degree," Connie said. "We tend to get comfortable with things a certain way and don't want to change."

"That was a bit of a problem for us when we became Christians," Tim said. "Even though we could see we needed to make changes in our lifestyle, it was difficult to actually do. Looking back, over the past several months, it seems kind of silly, I guess."

"But it seemed pretty serious at the time," Connie agreed. "Have you found that to be true for you?"

Josie was growing a bit uncomfortable. "I haven't really thought about it, I guess," she said. "I'm sure you're right and there are changes I need to make but I don't even know what they are yet. I'm just so."

"Well, don't worry about it, Josie. God will show you anything He wants you to do differently. Just wait for Him to lead you. You may not have that much to deal with," Tim assured her. "He'll let you know."

"OK. This is all so totally new for me. I didn't go to church more than five or six times in my life until I moved here.

"Tim's right, Josie. God will show you so don't worry about it. But you do need to be open to His leading." Connie said softly. "Come on, Tim, let's show Josie our huge back yard."

Tim grinned. "Yeah, come on, Josie, you gotta see this!"

They all stood up and followed Connie outside the back door. Josie didn't know whether to laugh or not, but it was surely the smallest backyard she'd ever seen. It couldn't have been more than fifteen feet from their back door to the end of the fence and, from side to side wasn't more than ten feet.

She glanced at Tim and Connie's faces and saw them ready to laugh.

"Well, it is rather large. However, will you fill it? Plant an orchard?"

They burst into laughter.

"When we looked at the house, we liked it right away," Connie confided. "But when we looked out the back door, we couldn't believe it."

"Yeah," Tim added, "we thought it was a joke of some kind."

"The lady showing us the house said the previous owners had been quite old and unable to get around much so didn't want a big yard to take care of," Connie said.

"But they still wanted a 'real yard' so they just had this little one. I guess they just sold off the rest of the land that went with it."

Josie just looked at the miniature yard and laughed again. "So, what are you going to do with it?"

"We're actually trying to see if it's at all possible to buy back some of the additional land. It seems to be part of the field of flowers out there, but we haven't been able to contact the owner." Tim pointed to the far-right corner and said, "Don't you see our award-winning sun flowers over there?"

"Yes, and my awesome day lily in the other corner?" Connie added.

"It surely is a small yard," Josie agreed.

After briefly discussing the upcoming Bible class on Tuesday and thanking her new friends for their hospitality, Josie took her leave. They seemed so happy together and confident that they were loved by the Lord. Even that silly little yard didn't upset them; they'd try to fix it but weren't worrying about it in the meantime. This, then, seemed to be some of that peace in action. Very appealing.

MONDAY MORNING WAS MORE hectic than usual, and Josie remembered how she and her dad would joke about it. She was more and more sure that he was wrong. The Christians she'd met didn't seem to have lost touch with reality at all. In fact, they may have had a better understanding of it than most others.

Every time Scott started to tell Josie about a job, the phone rang again. Finally, he handed her the clipboard, pointed to some pertinent information on the top couple of tickets, and waved her out the door.

Josie ran from job to job to job the entire day. By 5:30 she was on her way back to the shop for the last time that day. She hoped, anyway.

When she walked in the shop Scott was talking on the phone and writing on a work ticket. Josie figured there would be enough work for to-morrow from the looks of it. This was a tourist town and a lot of the calls for today had been for motels and restaurants who just had little things go wrong and wanted them fixed by yesterday.

Josie flopped down on a chair and just sat there. She wanted a soda from the machine, but it was at least five steps away. She'd wait. She heard Scott hang up the phone and swiveled around to face him. Before either of them could say a word, the phone rang again. Scott just shook his head, wiped his brow, and picked up the receiver.

Josie wondered how long this call would take. She suspected if she didn't get home and into the shower right away, she'd end up collapsing on her bed, still in her dirty clothes, and waking up that way the next morning. She stood up. She'd talk to Scott in the morning. She waved and, when he nodded his head in acknowledgment, she went home.

At home her landlady had put a note on her door letting her know that there would be a cold cuts, fruit and vegetables and iced tea for supper.

Josie made a pass through the dining room picking up her favorites from the platters on the table and went straight back to her room. Taking a few strawberries from the plate, she shed her dirty clothes and turned on the water in the shower. By the time the water was ready, the strawberries were gone. The shower somewhat rejuvenated her, so she managed to eat the rest of the food she'd brought. Well, most of it, anyway. Didn't quite get that broccoli eaten! Sorry, Dad.

TUESDAY AFTERNOON FOUND JOSIE nearly as tired as she'd been the day before. But, today, she knew she had Bible class that night, so she kept trying to convince herself she was fine. It wasn't that the work was too much for her; she was only 24 and in good physical condition. Part of it was the heat and not sleeping at night. Part of it was the frantic pace things had been the past couple of weeks. But a big part of it, Josie thought, is the lie. It's killing me.

ONE OF THE THINGS that came up in the Bible class that night was that we need to have our relationships with other people in good standing. "In other words," PJ said, "if you're in a relationship of any kind that is based on a lie, untruth, misinformation, or the such, you need to get that cleared up."

"What do you mean, 'cleared up'?" someone asked.

"I mean that our relationships, all of them, work, friends, lovers, family, all need to be based on honesty. You cannot really have a true relationship with someone if there is a lie in the way," PJ said.

There was other conversation, but Josie didn't hear it. PJ's words kept echoing in her head. Her relationship with Scott was based on a lie. Actually, her relationship with everyone here in Rapid City was based on a lie. What was she to do?

When the class was dismissed, Josie stayed behind to see if PJ had time to talk with her. She was afraid if she didn't do this right away, she'd never get the nerve. Perhaps then she'd just have to leave town.

"OK, JOSIE. EVERYONE'S GONE so why don't we sit back down, and you can tell me what's on your mind."

"I've screwed everything up, I'm afraid," Josie said, lips quivering
"You see, everything is a lie."

"A lie?"

Josie nodded her head.

"Why don't you start at the beginning, Josie," PJ said kindly.

"I'm a girl."

"Pardon?"

"I'm a girl."

"A girl?"

Josie nodded again, but now tears had started down her cheeks and she didn't seem to be able to stop them. Frustrated, she swiped at them, but they kept coming.

"Josie? Can you explain?"

Haltingly, Josie stammered out her story. PJ just nodded from time to time, but his eyes never left hers. He handed her a box of facial tissues but didn't interrupt her. ". . .so, now I don't know what to do."

They discussed the situation at some length, but the fact was that Josie was going to have to talk to Scott, first, and everyone else who'd befriended her and let them know the truth. "After you get things right with God."

"Oh! Is He mad at me, too?"

"He's not mad, Josie. He loves you. But this is sin and you need to ask His forgiveness. 1 John 1:9 says that if we confess our sin, He is faithful and just to forgive us our sin and to cleanse us from all unrighteousness. But you need to confess it. Do you understand that?"

Josie was uncertain. "What does confess mean, PJ?"

"It means we tell Him we know we did something wrong and ask him to forgive us for it. Make sense?"

"I guess. If we don't do it, then aren't we really Christians?"

"He has forgiven all of our sin, past, present and future so He's not going to unforgive us. Our standing with Him does not change; we are His children. But our relationship is affected. You know if you've had a disagreement with someone you don't feel quite reconciled to them or comfortable with them until you discuss the problem. This is the same thing. We just need to feel free to come to Him and we don't if we know we've done something wrong."

"So, it's more for us than for Him?" Josie asked.

"Right. Do you want me to pray with you, Josie?"

"Yes, please. I don't really know how yet."

PJ led her in a prayer of confession and explained more about 'keeping short accounts with God'. Then he told her she needed to talk to Scott right away.

"Do you think he will be mad?"

"Josie, I don't have any idea how he will react. But you must realize that he has more reason than anyone else to be upset with you. You've deceived him on a daily basis for several weeks and he is also bound to feel a bit, well, a bit stupid. . . you know, for not realizing it."

"Do you think he'll fire me?"

"Josie. I don't know. But I don't think that's your first priority."

"I know. It's just that I need this job, or I'll have to go back home."

"Josie, I think you need to set things right with Scott, regardless of your job. You have wronged him greatly and you need to be very careful to make his feelings a much higher priority than your job." PJ said very sternly.

"I guess I sound like a ninny. I do know Scott has every right to be upset with me. It just seemed so harmless when I started. I know many women did that during the war years because they didn't think they would be hired otherwise. No one has ever acted like that was such a big deal so I didn't realize this would be so bad."

"Josie, did you talk this over with your parents before you came down here?"

"Well, my dad told me he didn't think it was such a great idea but only because he didn't think I could pull it off."

"What about your mom?"

"She's been gone for years."

"Oh, Josie. I'm sorry. What did she die from?"

"She didn't die. She left." Josie thought she was past this thing about her mother, but it was threatening to reduce her to tears again. She shook her head and angrily wiped at her eyes. "She's just gone."

"Do you want to talk about it?"

"No!"

"Okay. Sorry. But if you ever do, please remember that I'm here."

"I'm sorry, PJ. I just thought I was past crying any tears over her but lately it seems to happen a lot. It's very frustrating."

"Maybe you need to talk it out and deal with it. You probably didn't ever do that, did you?"

"No. Dad didn't want us talking about her and we were scared and mad at her so that was fine with us."

"But perhaps you do need to talk about it now. Not necessarily tonight but soon," PJ said gently.

"Okay. But I need to go home now. I have to figure out how I'm going to talk to Scott about this. Plus, it's been so busy this week I haven't even been able to say hello and good-bye, so I don't know how I'll get a chance to talk to him about this."

"Perhaps you should call him at home and arrange to meet with him."

"If it's crazy busy tomorrow I'll try to set up something with him, I promise."

PJ said a short prayer with Josie and said he'd be praying for her. Giving her a quick hug, he reminded her, "I'm here if you need me."

As Josie drove home, she knew it was going to take a lot of prayer. She'd wanted to be free from the lie, but she hadn't realized how hard it could really get. But it was too late to turn back now.

WHEN JOSIE WALKED IN the next morning Scott was on the phone, again (or still?), and he grinned and waved. Josie waved but she wasn't grinning. She'd hardly slept the night before for trying to figure out how to do this. The more she thought about it the harder she decided it was going to be.

"Earth to Josie! Earth to Josie! Earth to Jo. . .. Oh, there you are, Josie. I wasn't sure you were actually here." Scott laughed.

"Oh, sorry. Guess my mind was elsewhere," Josie apologized.

"Like on Mars, maybe?" Scott teased.

"Something like that. Scott, I need to talk to you about something important," Josie said quickly, before she lost her nerve.

"Okay. This sounds serious," Scott said, looking worried. "Is something wrong?"

"Yeah. Me!" Josie blurted. "I've done something awful. You're going to hate me!"

"Josie, what did you do? Rob a bank?"

"No. I lied!"

"About what? To me?"

"About me. Yes, to you."

"Josie! Tell me! You're scaring me."

"Scott, I'm a girl!"

"Yeah! Right! Come on, Josie! Be serious."

"I am."

"Serious?"

"Yes. And a girl!" Josie whipped off her long-sleeved work shirt to reveal a very feminine looking upper body dressed in a tank top, and pulled her hair back so her face really showed up.

"Oh, my goodness! You are a girl!"

"Like I've been saying."

"But, why? I don't understand. Are you hiding from someone?"

"I did it, in the beginning, because I didn't think I could get a job anywhere if they knew I was a girl. I'm qualified and trained but most places won't even talk to a girl about this kind of a job. Several contractors in Montana just laughed at me when I tried to apply for work. If you're a guy, people just seem to assume you know what you're doing."

"But, Josie, why didn't you tell me? Didn't you think you could trust me?"

"It's just that, once you start a lie, it gets harder and harder to get out of it. I've been miserable for weeks but just didn't know how to stop it. This lie is destroying me. And now you probably hate me."

"No. I don't hate you. I don't really know how I feel. This is such a shock. I think I need time to figure it all out." Scott suddenly realized the phone was ringing. As he moved to answer it, his answering service picked it up. "I didn't hear it ringing."

"I kind of heard it in the background, I think. Maybe more than once." Josie was shaking and reaching for a chair.

"I guess. Hey, you all right?" Scott started toward Josie, but she held up her hand.

"I'm okay. I just needed to sit."

The phone started ringing again. This time Scott reached for it, grabbed a work order and pen and spoke into the phone, "Scott's Handyman Service. How may I help you?"

Josie didn't hear a word he said. She wasn't shaking anymore. Just sort of numb. 'I wonder what happens now', she thought. 'I've just gotten myself fired and lost a good friend'. She leaned forward, placing her elbows on her knees and burying her face in her hands. 'what am I going to do? God, are you here?"

"ARE YOU OKAY?" SCOTT touched her lightly on her shoulder as he spoke. She sat up quickly, almost jumping.

"Yeah. I'm fine. I guess you want me to leave now," she said flatly, standing up. "I'll check my truck for any of your tools or supplies." She started toward the door.

"Josie? I don't know how I feel about all of this. But I do know you're a good worker and I'd like for you to stay, at least for now, if you're willing."

She stopped. "Really?"

"Yeah. I need the help and you've been doing a good job."

"Okay. I like working for you and I'd like to stay. At least, until you decide to fire me." She tried to smile but it didn't quite reach her face.

Scott gave her a couple of work tickets and she loaded up and left. Luckily, both jobs looked relatively simple and she was grateful. She wasn't sure how good her brain would work today, and she sure didn't need to mess anything else up.

As she'd anticipated, the jobs were simple, and she was soon on her way back to the shop. She'd teased Scott about not just calling her with more work or letting her call in for her next assignment. But, after they tried the cell phone at the beginning, Scott liked his system the way they were doing it. Said he had a better idea of how things were going when she checked back in with him through out the day. But this time, she'd sure rather be able to call in for the next job. She wasn't quite ready to face Scott yet, and was a little fearful that, as he had time to think it over, he might change his mind about letting her stay on.

She drove past the church and then turned back and went in. "PJ, do you have a quick minute?" she asked, sticking her head in the door of his office.

"Why, yes, Josie. Come in. How's it going?"

"I told Scott this morning."

"Good. How did that go?"

"Well, I'm still alive and still employed but I don't know for how long. I think he took it pretty well, but he was so shocked that I don't think even he knows how he feels about it."

"It may take a while. You may find that he starts to become angry and withdrawn as the full implications of this really sink in. Be prepared to give him plenty of time," PJ counseled.

"Thanks, PJ. I have to get going. I was driving by and decided to run in real quick and let you know where I am."

"I'm glad you did. I'm praying for you, Josie."

"I'm counting on it." Josie waved. "Thanks."

Scott looked up as the door opened. He hadn't heard Josie pull in but there he, rather she, stood. He checked the ticket in his hand and realized, by the call time he'd noted, that he'd been holding it for at least twenty minutes. Just standing there. This was just all too much.

"Hi, Scott."

"Josie." Scott picked up his stack of tickets, sorted through them and gave three of them to Josie. "These should get done next. I expect they're all pretty straight forward, simple jobs. Thank God for that."

"Right." Josie looked over the tickets, asked Scott a question on one of them, took the supplies she'd need and left.

He hadn't been really friendly, but he hadn't shot her. So far, so good.

By the time she came back in Scott's disposition had taken an even more ominous turn. He barely acknowledged her presence, handing her more job tickets, briefly explaining a request on one then returning to his own work on a chair he was building to match others in a customer's dining room set.

The atmosphere at the end of the day was rather neutral with Scott just saying, "Good night. See you in the morning."

Josie just nodded her head and left. This was going to be a real long week. She had thought she might try to call Connie and Tim and see if they had time to talk with her either Wednesday or Thursday. But, seeing how hard this all was with Scott she lost her nerve. Maybe she'd better deal with one person at a time. Or, if things didn't work out with Scott and she had to leave town, she might just never worry about the others. What would it matter?

Chapter 8

THE REST OF THE week seemed to move in slow motion. Scott was civil to Josie but that was it. Friday night when Josie left all Scott said was," see ya."

As Josie left, she had mixed feelings. No game to go to tonight and pretend to enjoy. But right now, I'd trade several baseball games for a friendly exchange with Scott again. I sure miss our easy camaraderie, his silly grin, and giving him a bad time. Wonder if we'll ever be friends again.

I think I'd like much more but right now I'd settle for friends. Boy, I really messed stuff up.

The weekend stretched before her like an ocean. What was she to do with it? She'd gotten used to the Friday night game and then hanging out with Scott for a while. Then there's Sunday, she thought. I'm supposed to go to his folks for dinner. That's out, now. Oh, yeah. And what am I supposed to wear to church? If I go in a dress, or even slacks and a shirt, would anyone recognize me? What if they do? What if they don't?

Boy, that little lie is costing me more and more, as each day goes by.

Maybe I should just load up and head for Montana. All Dad would say is that he told me I couldn't do it. He'd put me right back to work and we could just pretend none of it mattered. Then she heard a little voice that reminded her that the reason it was a problem here is that she'd become a Christian and living a life based on lies was not the right thing to do.

She wanted her dad to accept Jesus as his savior, just as she had. If she went home now, with all of this unresolved, he'd never be open to the Word of God. So, guess I have to stay and face the music. Sighing, she parked her truck and went into the rooming house. No signs of supper anywhere.

Guess she'd have to go get something if she wanted to eat. Hot and tired, she debated if food was even worth the effort.

SCOTT SHOWED UP AT Star of the West sports complex looking like he'd just lost his best friend. Indeed, perhaps he had. These past few days had been full of bitterness and betrayal and he felt he'd never, ever been deceived to such an extent. Even when Stacie dumped me for the dude with the fancy car, he recalled. That had hurt but as he'd watched her romance flourish but then disintegrate, he was able to see aspects of her character that had also affected his relationship with her. As he faced those truths, the pain had begun to slip away. He'd moved on, determined to be wiser in the future and he had, with the fairer gender, anyway.

But nothing prepared him for the sense of loss this situation with Josie had flooded him with. I guess I pretty much took her at face value, he thought. It never occurred to me to question who she said she was. So, that makes me part of the problem, doesn't it? Too dumb to watch out for myself, he muttered as he locked his truck and headed toward the field.

"Hey, Scott," their pitcher greeted him. "Why the sad face?"

Resolutely pasting a smile on his face, Scott looked up. "Hi, Roger, what did you say?"

"I questioned your sad puppy dog face," Roger replied. "That phony grin doesn't cut it with me. I've known you too long."

Forcing a lightness he didn't feel, Scott responded by hitting Roger in the arm and continued toward the field. "I'm fine. Just your imagination, Rog."

Other teammates didn't actually call him on it but he sensed, rather than felt, their questioning eyes on him throughout the game. Glad when it was over, he escaped as quickly as he could. He sure wasn't ready to talk about Josie. How could he try to tell someone else about something he still hadn't figured out? But he wished he could talk to someone about it. Maybe it would help him sort out his feelings. He thought about going over to his folks' but decided there'd probably be too much going on there for a private conversation.

Bypassing the small hamburger joint the team often congregated at after their games, Scott headed directly home. Guess I'll mow the grass, he contemplated. Needs to be cut and this is as good a time as any. Besides, the roar of the motor allowed him to just put his brain in neutral and not think at all. Thinking is my problem, he decided. If I could stop thinking about this mess it wouldn't hurt so bad.

Why in the world did she feel she had to lie to me? I'm a fair guy. I'd have given her a shot. But then, even over the noise of the mower he heard a small voice asking, are you sure?

Well, yeah, he told himself. I'd have given her the job and, once I'd checked a few jobs, I'd have kept her on. Now the voice seemed louder. Would you have? Or would you have seen that she was a girl, not a very big one, either, or decided she wasn't strong enough to do the work? Or, maybe people would laugh at you for hiring a girl. Would you really have given her a chance?

The debate raged as he finished with the mower and got out the weed clipper. By the time he was through, had put his tools away, and hopped into the shower, all he was certain about was that he didn't truly know how he would have treated Josie if she'd applied as herself. Maybe she's right, he thought. Maybe that really was the only way she could get a job. She's really very qualified and experienced and an excellent worker. Maybe his gender was incapable of acknowledging a woman's abilities in previously male dominated jobs. What if she really is right? What kind of man does that make me?

He watched the news and wearily made his way to his room. If he could only sleep and forget, at least he wouldn't be so tired. He caught himself whining about the heat then reminded himself that he, at least, had air conditioning and that Josie was suffering with nothing more than a fan.

Josie again!! Couldn't he get that woman out of his mind at all? Apparently not, he grumbled. Apparently not.

SATURDAY EVENING JOSIE PLACED her customary phone call to her dad. He immediately sensed her despair and coaxed the story out of her. Since she wanted him to be open to Jesus, she didn't tell him how bitter Scott was, just said he was having some trouble absorbing the news. As they talked, Josie surprised herself by mentioning her mother. "Dad, do you have any idea where she is?"

"Why would I?" he replied. "I told you, she left us, all three of us. We're better off without her."

But Josie sensed something she'd never heard before. "I know. But, maybe she started missing us after she'd been gone for a while. Would you have let her come back?"

"No."

"Why, Dad? Didn't you love her?"

"Of course, I did, when we got married anyway. But when she left, she killed it. I don't ever want to see her again," he said vehemently. "I don't want to talk about her either."

Apologizing for upsetting him, Josie said good-bye and hung up the phone. That's strange, she thought, it really sounded like I touched a nerve. I'm sure that's never happened before. Wonder if he knows more than he's telling us girls? But why would he have kept their mom away from them if she'd tried to come back? Why did she leave, actually? He'd only said she'd left them and didn't want them anymore. Why?

Josie took her dirty clothes down the hall to the washing machine and watched the machine fill. As her clothes swished around in the sudsy water, she tried to read the Bible she'd brought with her. The chapter she was reading was in John, of course. This was her second time through, and she enjoyed it, it seemed very reassuring and comforting and full of love, but she had to admit she didn't really understand some of it.

But in this verse in the fourteenth chapter Jesus said that if we ask anything in His name, He would do it. Did He mean that? Could He fix this mess she'd made? Could He find her mother? Did she really want to find her mother? Until these past few days she'd never really considered it. Or had she? Maybe, deep down, she'd always wanted to find Pamela.

Well, she reasoned most people want to know their mother, don't they? After all, I should know her health history for my own sake. What if I need that information some day and it's not available? No, I should try to find her and get that data before it's too late. But what if I find her and she doesn't want anything to do with me? After all, she left us. Oh well, I can just get the health info and get right back out of her life. Just like she, obviously, wants it. I guess.

As she put her clothes in the dryer, Josie's mind wandered to Scott's family. His mom was so nice; his whole family was really a loving, teasing, nurturing group. How she envied them. Did they have any idea how lucky they were? They'd accepted her so openly, been so nice to her. How would they treat her now? Had she completely lost their good will, their friendship? And what about Connie and Tim? Would they be able to forgive her deception? Figured that she'd blow it with someone who wanted to be friends with her. Story of her life.

What was she to do about church tomorrow? If Scott had told his family about her, they'd be sure to think she was stupid to show up in her guy clothes. But if he hadn't, that might not be the best place to try to explain herself to them. Could she go as herself, slip in late, sit toward the back and leave during the final prayer? I don't want to miss, she thought. I need to learn as much as I can.

Back in her room, she folded her clothes and put them away. When she caught herself putting a pair of her work sox in her jewelry box, she knew her mind just wasn't on her chores. Carefully, she retraced her steps and retrieved a few other things she'd put in the wrong place.

She drifted off to sleep sometime after midnight. The last time she looked at the clock it said five after twelve. She woke up several times during the night, restless and uncomfortable from the heat. Her dreams were disturbing and involved something bad happening to Scott or his family. One that she remembered when she awoke had been vague but seemed to be about a woman she couldn't see clearly. Mom? Hmm, I haven't dreamed about her for years. Since I stopped crying myself to sleep at night, she recalled. I wonder if she ever cried herself to sleep over me.

Sometime during the night her mind had decided she should go to church as herself and slip in and out unnoticed. Grateful that she could wear summer clothes and be more comfortable, she acknowledged to herself that she was also scared to death. What if someone recognized her?

But I'm not going to miss church. I need to be there; there's so much I don't know. Nervously, she accepted a bulletin from an usher and wordlessly indicated that she'd prefer sitting in the empty pew in the back. One of the worship choruses they sang was familiar to her from previous services and she timidly joined her voice with theirs. It felt good to be herself. But, what a price!

When the congregation stood for the closing hymn she slipped out and drove away quickly. No sense in making things worse. Oh, no! She was supposed to go for dinner with Scott's family. She drove straight home, called Scott's mom's number and, using her 'guy' voice, left a message that she was ill and unable to attend church and dinner. As she hung up she realized that, again, she was dealing with the situation by lying.

I don't remember having trouble telling the truth before, she thought.

Here I am, supposed to be a follower of Jesus, and I'm still not telling the truth. I wonder how many mistakes like this I can make before He kicks me out. I need to talk to PJ again.

The bulletin only gave the phone number to the church, so she tried to find him in the city phone book. Wonder if this is him? The address was on Evergreen drive, which she thought was out in the west side of the city. Well, it's worth a try. She waited until 1:30 and then placed her call. PJ agreed to meet her at the church at three that afternoon. She paced the floor of her room and finally moved her activity outside and walked around a few blocks. She knew that if someone who was supposed to be her friend had lied to her as much as she had been doing, she'd have washed her hands of them long ago. Sure hope Jesus is more forgiving than I'd be, she thought. At 2:45 she got in her truck and drove to the church. PJ was just unlocking the door so she hopped out and joined him inside.

"I'm having a real bad time with this situation," she began. "Never realized a lie could cause so much trouble."

"Yes. They tend to take on a life of their own," he agreed. "What, in particular, is the biggest problem right now?"

Josie filled him in on the past few days with Scott and the awareness that she was lying about other things, like the phone message to Scott's mom about dinner earlier that day. "Will God just get sick of my messing up all the time and kick me out?"

"No. He's pretty patient with us. Like we talked before, you need to acknowledge to Him that you've failed, which He already knows, and accept His forgiveness. Then you move on and, with His help, you do better."

Relieved, Josie smiled and relaxed a bit. Then she told him about the phone conversation with her father. "This is the first time I've wondered if he was telling me the total truth about my mom," she confided. "But I haven't really expressed any interest in years so maybe it was the surprise of me asking about her."

As PJ asked questions, Josie filled him in on what little she actually remembered about her mother. Pamela had left when Josie was seven and her sister, Hope, was nine. Their father, Sam, had simply told the girls that their mother was gone and wouldn't be returning. When the girls had cried, he'd been rather harsh, telling them that he wanted to hear no tears for someone who didn't want them anymore. They'd learned quickly not to ask about her or talk about her when he was there. Initially, they'd talked about her between themselves but gradually even that had ended.

Sam had been mom and dad to them, taking treats to school for special occasions, attending PTA meetings, teaching them to shop and do the housekeeping chores. Some of the more feminine problems had been difficult until Sam's sister moved to town and made herself available to the girls. "She was always there for us," Josie recalled. "We learned we could ask her anything," She giggled. "Sometimes she didn't know the answers, but she'd bravely do the best she could."

"I'm sure she was a real blessing to you both," PJ said with a smile. "What did she think of your plan to come down here?"

Josie just looked at the floor for a moment. "Aunt Helen died two years ago."

"I'm sorry to hear that. Was she ill?"

"No, killed by a drunk driver."

"That's too bad. The loss is difficult enough but the anger at the other driver can destroy you. Have you dealt with that?"

"Yes. Well, maybe not. We did talk about it a lot when it happened. But a few months after the accident, Dad said he was tired of hearing about it and that it was time to move on."

"It must have been very difficult for him," PJ observed. "Perhaps hearing about it over and over was just too painful for him."

"I think you're right on that," Josie agreed. "We girls did a lot of crying and talking when Dad wasn't around, so I think we worked through it pretty well. But I don't know if Dad ever did."

"Back to what you said earlier, I take it you'd like to try to find your mother?"

"I think so. I'm surprised at myself, I never thought I would. I should probably at least find out about her health history and maybe I need more than that, too. But I have no idea how to start."

"Did she have any brothers or sisters?" PJ asked.

"I'm not sure. Oh, yes. I think I remember hearing about a brother. Adam, I think."

"Did you ever hear where your mother grew up? Was she from Montana?"

Josie struggled with the vague and faded memories she had of the days before Pamela had left. Finally, she remembered hearing something about Spearfish, but she didn't know who was there. Trying to remember her mother's maiden name was even harder. "I don't know if I ever heard it," she admitted. "If so, I was too young to pay attention."

"Yes. That's not a concept familiar to young children, anyway. What is your sister's middle name?" PJ asked.

"Hope's name is Hope Emerald."

"Do you think your mother's maiden name could have been Emerald?"

"I guess it's possible. I always thought her middle name was just the name of a gem because my middle name is Crystal,"

"And you could be correct." PJ reached for a phone book and checked the Spearfish section. No one named Emerald was listed. "Well, let's try your middle name."

They found two listings for Crystal and one for Chrystal. Neither was for Adam. "Could Adam be his middle name?" PJ wondered. "I see this one has initials, D.A. Chrystal. Do you think it's worth trying?"

Josie shrugged her shoulders. This was happening too fast. Not sure if she was ready to actually find someone who could tell her about her mother she stood up and gazed out the window.

"Josie? We don't have to go any further today. In fact, you don't ever have to follow up on this. It could be a dead end or it could lead you to something or someone. Do you want to wait?"

"I don't know. I want to know but this is really scary," Josie admitted. "I don't know what to say."

"It's up to you. If you'd like I can place the call. That way, we could see if this leads to anything and you could stop whenever you want," PJ offered.

Josie nodded. "If you don't mind," she said. "I'm not sure I could do it right now. PJ picked up the phone and dialed. Josie stood it as long as she could then bolted out of the room, down the hallway and outside to her truck. Leaning her head against the door she gave in to the tears that came, unbidden, and rolled down her face. This is a big mistake, she thought. I never should have talked about this. I'm opening Pandora's box.

"Josie?" PJ was beside her, touching her gently on her shoulder. "Are you okay?" She nodded but didn't look up. "The person I spoke with says Pamela is her sister-in-law. She said that Adam isn't home right now but seemed to think he'd welcome hearing from you."

Josie turned slowly to face PJ. "Really?"

"Yes, and then she said the strangest thing."

"What?"

"She said something about Pamela trying to reach you for years."

"Oh!" Josie just stared at PJ. "Do you suppose she really did? We are still where she left us so we should have been pretty easy to find."

"Is there any possibility that she tried and your father stopped things on that end?" PJ asked. "Something to consider."

"I just don't know. Well, I guess I should go. Oh, wait. Are you going to call that number again?"

"I can, if you'd like. In fact, if you want me to, I could meet with her and find out what the story really is. That way, you can decide if you want to pursue this or not without actually having to meet with her." PJ offered.

Josie paused to consider. "That might be very good. It would give me a chance to think over whatever you learn and be better prepared to meet her. Are you sure you don't mind?"

"I'd be happy to do this for you, Josie. Let me know what information I am free to share with her and I'll do the best I can."

"Thanks."

Chapter 9

SCOTT ARRIVED AT WORK early on Monday, giving him time to lay out the pieces for the new dining room table he was going to build for a long-time customer, Leona Saltzman. This dear lady wanted a copy of the table her parents had purchased, second hand, when she was a small child. She'd found pictures in her old photo albums and had loaned them to Scott. They were sort of guessing on the size, but Leona said if it was even close, she'd be happy.

Any other time, I could do this with my eyes shut, he thought. Why am I having difficulty now? He checked his work and realized he'd left an important part out, the pedestal for the table. Guess I'd better have that, he figured. Be kind of hard to use if it had to sit on the floor. Wherever is my mind?

On Josie, of course. She's due to arrive for work in just under an hour and I'm no more ready to face her than I was last week. He bowed his head. Dear Lord, he prayed, please help me with this. I'm angry and hurt and puzzled and frustrated. Yet, I know I really have no right to be upset with her, at least not to this extent. You are the one she sinned against. Sure, she lied to me. But aside from that, she's been an excellent employee and has created a lot of goodwill toward me through the way she's dealt with my customers. She's done me way better than harm. So why can't I get past this feeling that I'm the one who's been hurt? Please help me to see and understand what You want me to. Help me treat her right when she gets here. Father, I just really don't know how to react to her; guess that's part of the problem. I trust you to handle this for her and to help me process this and respond in the way that is pleasing to You. Thank you that you always hear my prayers and that you love me. Amen.

He went back to his drafting board and the plans seemed to materialize before his eyes. Okay, he thought. This is better. That's amazing, I didn't even ask for help with this, but God is so good. As he finished his sketches, he realized he was humming under his breath.

A few minutes later when Josie arrived Scott looked toward the door and greeted her with a smile. "Good morning, Josie. Ready for another hard week?"

She seemed relieved. I really was ugly last week, wasn't I? Wow. What does this say about me, Lord?

"Josie, I apologize for my rotten behavior last week. I'm sure this is all very difficult for you and I just made it harder."

"That's okay, boss. I got what I deserved."

"No. I acted like a boor and I really am sorry. Do you want to talk about any of this?"

Josie hesitated and Scott continued, "Not that you have to. But if you need a friendly shoulder, I'm available."

"Thanks, Scott. I really appreciate it. I'm terribly sorry about lying to you. Can you ever forgive me?"

"Josie, I have to be honest and admit I've had a real hard time with this, but I finally wised up and went to God with it. I won't say I'm not still bothered by it, but I figure that's more between you and God than between you and me."

"Yes. That's what PJ has been telling me," Josie agreed.

"PJ! You've been talking to him?"

"Yes. He's been a great help to me. In fact, he's the one who said I had to come clean about who I am."

"So, PJ knows all about this?"

"Yes. You see, I prayed with him a couple of weeks ago and I've been going to a Bible Study class on Tuesday nights for new believers. It was something he said in class last Tuesday that really upset me. I stayed and we talked. That's when I told him the truth."

"Josie! You became a believer? That's awesome!" Scott was really grinning now. "I've actually been praying for that since you started here. My mom, too. Does she know?"

"I doubt it. I think the only ones who know are just the people in the class. At least, I haven't told anyone else."

"I'm so glad to know that. I've been worried over the weekend that my reaction to all of this might turn you away from God."

After a few more minutes Josie walked toward the refrigerator. "I think we'd better get to work, don't you, Scott? It looks like you have a big pile of work tickets."

Scott grinned. "Yeah. Guess we'd better get busy. But will you promise me something?"

"What?"

"That if I start acting like a jerk again, you'll punch me in the nose?"

"Nope. Never punched anyone in the nose when I was pretending to be a guy. Sure, don't plan to as a gal."

Scott showed her the jobs he wanted her to get to right away and Josie loaded up and left. Scott watched her walk to her truck. Hmm, he thought. That's part of what was wrong. She walks like a girl. He continued watching her as she climbed into her truck and drove off. Yup. She's definitely a girl.

As he turned back to his work on the table and began sawing his wood to size, he felt himself smiling. What? he demanded, gruffly. But inside he knew that he was really glad to be back on good terms with Josie. Male or female, she'd become special to him.

JOSIE GRINNED AS SHE drove off toward Serendipity Place. This is sure better than last week, she thought. I really missed Scott. I didn't realize how much I've come to think of him as a very special guy. Maybe now that I can be myself, I can try to figure out exactly how special.

That week at work went well for both Scott and Josie. There was still a little bit of awkwardness brought on by the awareness, by both of them, that they were the opposite gender and very possibly interested in each other. But they also now knew they were fellow believers and that seemed to forge a new bond. They began talking about the Bible a little as Josie said she was now on her third time through John but saw something new every time she read it.

As time went by, they talked about her deception and how it affected others, friends at church and his family. Josie was more concerned about how his family would feel towards her than anything else although she wanted to have an honest, up-front relationship with those in her Bible class as well. After all, part of the learning process in the class involved people sharing their questions and thoughts and that just about demanded that they could trust each other. She might really have an uphill road there.

At PJ's urging Josie went to the class in a skirt and blouse. At first many of them thought she was a new person. She introduced herself as Josie and then, haltingly, told them the truth. Some of them didn't seem too affected but Connie and Tim were clearly stunned. Looking directly at them, Josie said, "I especially want to apologize to you guys. You've been so good to me and I really enjoyed my time with you. I'd hoped we could be friends but I'll understand if you want to back away, now."

Neither said anything and PJ started the Bible study. Josie felt torn; she wanted to learn as much as she could, but she was also feeling a real sense of loss. It was hard to stay focused. When class dismissed, she scooted out immediately and left, disappointed and yet knowing they had the right to be upset with her.

FRIDAY EVENING AS THEY left work both Scott and Josie expressed their appreciation for a much better week. They had discussed his family and Scott was going to talk to them that evening after his game, if they were home. If they responded favorably, Josie would stop by Saturday, at their convenience, and talk to them more and answer any questions they might have.

"I just feel like this is the coward's way out, Scott. Will they see it that way, too?" Josie worried. "I don't want to make this any worse than it already is."

"I really think I should break it to them first. I don't honestly think they'll be angry with you; more likely a little hurt."

"I hope you're right. I would sure love it if they can forgive me and not want to run me out of town." Josie smiled but the thought of having the Mayforths reject her nearly brought her to tears. "They've been so good to me."

Scott agreed to call her as soon as he left their house. Josie was too nervous to go back to her room, so she parked and started walking along the bike path by Memorial Park after she'd admired their awesome rose gardens. That, in itself, was soothing. There were a lot of walkers as well as bikers along the path and people were friendly, so she began to wind down a bit. When she realized she was nearly to the Baken Park Shopping Center she turned back. As she drove home her phone rang. It was Scott.

"Just a minute, Scott. Let me pull over so we can talk. I don't want to cause an accident." As she pulled into an empty parking space she said, "Okay. I'm ready. Tell me."

"It really went pretty well, Josie. They were surprised, yet I don't think my mom was as surprised as I'd thought she would be."

"Do you think she suspected me?" Josie asked.

"I don't know. Maybe. She didn't say but you might learn more when you talk to them. They'd like you to join them for lunch around one tomorrow. Can you make that?"

"Lunch? I'm not the main course, am I?"

"No, silly." Scott laughed. "But you could be dessert!."

'Scott!"

"Sorry. Couldn't resist."

"You didn't try."

"Not very hard, no," Scott admitted. "I'll call Mom and tell her you'll be there, okay?"

"Thanks. Maybe you should come, too?"

"Nope. I have my orders. I'm to stay out of it."

"That sounds scary."

Scott laughed, wished her luck, and hung up.

Josie sat there for a while, lost in thought. Was this good or bad that they wanted to see her? Couldn't be too bad if they wanted to feed her lunch, right? Like she'd be able to eat anything. She started up her truck and headed for her rooming house. Maybe now she could eat. Better swing by McDonalds and pick up something. Way too late for anything from her landlady.

Chapter 10

Josie's lunch with the Mayforths went well. They were very cordial to her and insisted they all relax and eat before starting to talk. But over the salads, fruit and tea much of Josie's story came out easily. As Jim and Barb listened Josie found herself telling them much more than she'd anticipated.

"So, Josie, your mother has been gone since you were seven?" Barb asked. "That must have been difficult for you and your sister."

Josie agreed. "Once Aunt Helen moved near us it was a lot easier."

"Yes, I'm sure having a woman around was a good thing. There are so many questions during your teen years and I'm sure they were hard for your father to answer."

"Yeah!" Josie laughed. "You have no idea of some of the crazy answers we got from him sometimes. I guess if he didn't know the answer, he just made something up. Sometimes the answers weren't even related to the questions we had asked."

"Sounds like something I'd do," Jim said, laughing. "I do pretty well with my boys, but the girls would sure be in trouble if I was all they had."

"But he did the best he could for us," Josie said. "At least I think he did."

"Whatever do you mean, Josie, dear?" Barb asked.

So, Josie told them about the phone call PJ had made. "I don't know if he's reached my mother or not. I'm kind of anxious but I don't want to bug him. I'm sure as soon as he knows something, he'll let me know."

"So, do you think she tried to stay in touch and your father prevented it?"

Josie looked at Jim. "I guess that's a possibility."

"How are you going to feel about him if that proves true?"

"I don't know. Hope and I grew up thinking he was the only one who cared about us; that our mom just left and never looked back. If she was trying to come back or at least communicate with us and Dad didn't let her, that's going to be hard to deal with." Josie paused. "You know, that's not something we even considered as a possibility. It never crossed our minds."

"Josie, if that proves to be the case, I hope you'll remember that he probably did what he truly thought was best for all of you," Barb counseled.

"I've thought about that a lot," Josie confessed. "I just can't imagine him doing that. I wish I could talk to Hope but I'm waiting until I hear back from PJ."

"This waiting must be very difficult for you," Barb said, sympathetically. "Especially when this current situation is so different than what you've always thought to be true."

"If I just knew, one way or the other," Josie said. "Not knowing is really hard. My mind just goes in circles all the time."

Jim looked thoughtful. "Josie, did PJ talk to you about 'committing it to the Lord'?"

Josie shook her head. "I don't know. Everything is so new to me and there's so much going on. I'm having trouble keeping it straight in my head."

"I'm sure he prayed with you over this situation, though, didn't he?" Barb interjected. "What Jim means is simply that you tell the Lord that you realize this is a situation that is completely out of your hands and that only He can take care of it and then tell Him that you're not going to worry about it. You're going to leave it in His hands to deal with."

"Kind of dumping a lot on Him, isn't it?" Josie said. "I mean, He didn't create the problem, my folks did."

"But Josie, He invites us to cast all of our cares on Him because he cares for us." Jim responded.

"Really? Even when someone else caused the problem?"

"Of course. Josie, He loves us so much more than we ever truly realize. He wants to take care of us. He wants to solve our problems, answer our questions."

"That's pretty amazing. He'll help us any time?"

"That's right," Barb assured her.

"What about when we cause the problem ourselves? Like me, now?"

"That, too." Jim smiled. "Actually, most of the time we've at least had a hand in causing our problems. If we couldn't go to Him because of that we'd be in bad shape."

Jim and Barb explained many things to Josie that helped reassure her of her heavenly Father's love. One thing seemed to lead into another until

Josie looked at her watch. "Oh, no! It's nearly four o'clock. I've wasted your whole afternoon!"

"Not wasted, Josie. We invited you and we've enjoyed our time with you a great deal."

"It's sure nice of you. I'm really sorry about deceiving you all."

"Don't worry about it. We all make mistakes. Some are just more noticeable that others." Barb smiled. "Now, you were supposed to come to dinner last Sunday but didn't. So how about joining us tomorrow?"

"Well," Josie hesitated. "Is everyone going to be here?"

"I'm sure we'll have a house full; we always do. But you've met everyone before so I'm sure you'd have a nice time," Jim responded.

"And, if you want us to, we'll explain to our other children for you."

"You wouldn't mind?"

"Not at all," Barb said. "Cindy and Terry will be here for supper tonight and we'll let them know. Brenda usually calls Saturday evening to verify our dinner plans as she often contributes some of the food. I can let her know that you're really one of us, now. You know, one of us girls, and a Christian."

Josie left feeling like she had better friends than she'd ever thought possible. They make me feel loved, she realized. Even more than Dad has through the years.

EVEN THOUGH IT WAS Saturday night, Josie was tempted to not place her weekly phone call to her dad. Her emotions were all mixed up and she needed to know the truth about her mother. Resolving to keep the conversation light and just tell her dad that Scott was handling things and that they'd gotten along fine all week, Josie dialed the number. She was relieved when the line was busy but knew she'd have to try at least once more. When she reached her dad, he seemed preoccupied and they talked only a couple of minutes before he said he was sorry, but he had to get some things done. With mixed emotions she just told him she loved him and would talk to him next week.

At church on Sunday no one in the congregation acted like there was anything different about Josie. Maybe they just think I'm a new girl, she thought. That would be good if they didn't all know what a ninny she'd been. Many folks greeted her, but she couldn't tell if they recognized her or not. Maybe it didn't matter to most of them.

As promised, she went to dinner with the Mayforths and enjoyed herself immensely. The food was delicious and the table conversation enjoyable. 'I could live like this' she thought. This was what she'd missed by growing up without a mother. Unbidden, a tear appeared in her eyes. She quickly got it under control but as she glanced toward Barb, she realized the tear had been observed. Barb just smiled kindly at her and that almost triggered a flood of real tears.

Josie looked away and regained her control. This was silly. She hadn't cried over her mother in years. No way was she going to start now.

Josie offered to help with dishes before Scott could get up. At first it seemed Barb would insist she relax since she was a guest, but Barb smiled and said she'd welcome the help. After the table was cleared, the dishwasher loaded and most of the pans were dried and put away, Barb looked Josie directly in the face and asked, "So, Josie, what did you think about PJ's sermon this morning? You seemed quite interested."

"Oh, yes. I have so much to learn. Sometimes it all just seems to swirl around in my head, looking for a place to land. But sometimes, like yesterday with you and Jim, it just fits right into my mind and makes sense."

"There's a lot to learn," Barb agreed. "But you know, our Father knows where each of us is and has no expectations beyond that. As we learn more, He expects more of us. But even then, He helps us do whatever is required of us."

They joined the family in the living room. They had found a soccer match on TV and were rooting for the American women's team as they played a qualifying match for the World Cup.

"Josie, do you know soccer?" Brenda asked.

"Some," Josie admitted. "I played when I was younger."

"Did you know the American women won the first Women's World Cup in China?"

"No. I hadn't heard that."

"It was in 1991." Brenda grinned. "Shortly thereafter I saw tee shirts that said, 'Real men play soccer. . .. real women win the World Cup.' Not totally fair to our men but kind of funny, anyway."

Josie watched with them for a few minutes before thanking her hosts and taking her leave. As she walked to her truck, Barb walked out and put her hand on her arm. "Josie, if you need to talk, about any of this, or anything else, please call me." Josie nodded, overtaken with gratitude for such caring people.

When she got back to her room, she finished folding her clothes and put her laundry soaps away. Now that she could wear real clothes away from work, it seemed she had more laundry to do. Oh, well, she thought. I'm not complaining. Especially in this heat. It had gotten to 105 yesterday and in the high 90s today. Oh well, like they say in Arizona, it's a dry heat.

Chapter 11

AFTER THE SUN WENT down it cooled off a little so Josie took her Bible and went to sit on the porch swing. There was a cool breeze and the view of her landlady's flower gardens was very soothing. She turned to her place in John and was absorbed in her reading when her cell phone rang. It was PJ and he wanted to get together with her if she had time.

"Now?"

"If that works for you, Josie. If not, we'll set something else up."

"Now would be fine. Shall I meet you at the church?"

As she went back to her room to replace her Bible and get her truck keys she tried not to think about the implications of the call from PJ. I'll just wait and see what he says, she determined, but it was hard to keep her mind from circling like an eagle. PJ pulled into the church parking lot just as she did. She met him at the door of the church, and they went into his office.

"What's up?" Josie asked.

"I've just come from a meeting with your mother, Pamela," he explained. "I have a lot to tell you, but I want you to know that this is still entirely in your hands. I have her address and phone number to give you, but she has no knowledge of your location. I said I'd been contacted by you so didn't even let her know you're in Rapid City."

Josie let out a breath. "Thanks, PJ. But what did you find out?"

PJ gave her a shortened version saying she could get the details from Pamela if she decided to go that way.

Pamela had gone back to Spearfish to see her ailing mother after she and Sam had a big argument about it. After her mother died, he didn't want her to come back and when she did, he sent her away. At first, he'd let her talk to the girls occasionally and let her send cards on birthdays and Christmas.

Pamela had started going to church and became a Christian. This made her even more determined to reunite with her family, but Sam was adamant that she would not be allowed in their lives. Finally, Sam divorced her, and she didn't contest it. But after that he returned her cards to the girls and refused to let her speak to them.

Eventually Pamela had remarried and had two children, a boy and a girl who were now eight and ten.

"I have another sister and a brother?" Josie interrupted.

"Yes," PJ said gently. "I saw pictures of them."

"And a stepfather?"

"Yes. I didn't meet anyone except Pamela. We met in a restaurant to talk. She, of course, didn't bring anyone with her."

"Does she want to see me?"

"Very much. She cried when I didn't have a picture of you for her to see."

"I didn't even think of that," Josie said. "But I don't know if I have any pictures of me or Hope with me. We never took too many pictures. Dad said it was a waste of film since we still looked pretty much the same."

"It's okay. I know she would have loved to see pictures. But she was so happy to have a chance to get together with you. She said she finally gave up calling and sending cards when Sam wouldn't let anything go through."

"That really bothers me. He's lied to Hope and me all these years!"

Josie was crying. "He let us think she didn't care about us anymore. How could he do that?"

"I don't know, Josie. You'll have to talk to him about that. But remember, Pamela's story is just one side. You won't know the whole story until you hear your dad's side."

"You're right. PJ, I think I'd like my mom's info, now. I want to call Hope and let her know what I've found out, at least. We need to set something up to talk to our dad."

"Certainly. You might want to talk to Pamela and let her fill you in on her story. I didn't want to give you too much information at one time."

"That's a good idea. I'll try to call her first. Thank you, PJ. You don't know how much I appreciate your doing this for me." Josie stood to leave, wiping the remaining tears from her cheeks. "And for all your help in the rest of my life, too." She smiled. "I've really made a mess of things. You've helped me more than you could know."

Back in her room, where she'd have a good supply of tissues, Josie dialed the number for Pamela. When a woman answered Josie took a deep breath and said, "Is this Pamela?"

"Yes, it is."

"Mom? This is Josie."

They both cried too much to talk for several minutes. Finally, Josie heard Pamela's story: her mother had been having health problems and was getting older and Pamela determined she should spend a few weeks at home with her. Sam had heard that an old high school boyfriend of Pamela's was back in Spearfish, so he thought that was the real reason for the trip. He wanted her to just go for a weekend and then come right back.

They argued and she left during the night. She left their car at the bus terminal with a note on the seat. When she got to Spearfish, she called him, but he refused to speak with her. Over the next three weeks her mother seemed to get better then suddenly got worse and died. Pamela stayed on a while longer to help her sisters take care of their mother's house and belongings. She called Sam every week, but he was very angry and wouldn't let her speak to the girls. When she was ready to return to Montana, he told her to stay where she was, that he needed time to think. Finally, after a couple more weeks, she'd taken a bus back to Billings, Montana and hired a taxicab to get home. Sam had come home to fix his lunch and found her there. He ordered her out. Said she'd made her choice when she went to Spearfish to be with her old beau. She tried to make him understand that she'd gone for her mother and had only even seen the man in question once at the hospital.

"Josie, I tried. I really did try. But I wasn't a Christian then and I'm sure my temper got in the way of my good sense at times. I probably didn't do all I should have. By the time I became a Christian and tried to make things right, too much time had passed, and Sam felt there was no going back for us. That's when he sent me divorce papers. I didn't sign them for months, but he'd call and yell at me until I finally decided it was accomplishing nothing to refuse so I signed and sent them to him. The only thing I heard after that was when he sent me a copy of the finalized divorce."

Josie was quiet, trying to figure everything out. Was that when Sam had gone out and gotten so drunk? She only remembered it because she and Hope found him on the front porch passed out and it scared them so much.

It had only happened that once; otherwise she never knew her father to take a drink.

"Josie?"

"Oh, sorry, Mom. I was thinking about something that happened when I was about ten and wondering if that's when you got divorced."

"Josie, where is Hope?"

"She's going to college in Missoula. She worked for a few years after high school because she didn't know what she wanted to do. She's going to be a nurse."

"Will she speak to me, do you think?" Pamela's voice sounded so sad that Josie struggled with her tears.

"I haven't told her anything, yet. I'll call her and let her know I've found you and that you didn't just desert us. I think she'll want to talk to you."

"Josie? Where are you, dear?"

"Me? Oh, that's right. You don't know. I'm in Rapid City. I have a job that I really like. And. . .. Mom, I've become a Christian, too. But just a few weeks ago."

Now Pamela was crying. "I'm so glad. I've prayed for all three of you for so many years."

"Well, Dad and Hope don't know, yet. I've been waiting either for more courage or for a better time to tell Dad." She laughed at herself. "I'm not exactly the bravest person in the world and there's so much I still don't understand. I figured I'd better learn more before I try to argue with Dad."

"Perhaps you won't have to argue with him at all," Pamela suggested. "If he sees a change in you that may speak much louder than any words."

"Yeah. Well, I've made such a mess of things right now that I don't even want to try to talk to him until I've a better handle on things."

When Pamela asked, Josie filled her in on her summer, her job, her boss and PJ, and all of his help.

"I'm so glad you have him to talk to. He seemed like a very nice, compassionate man."

"Yes. He's been a lifesaver for me. I don't know what I'd have done without his wise counsel."

Josie gave Pamela her address and cell phone number and arranged to meet her the next weekend in Rapid City. With her work schedule plus her children and Josie's work schedule and her Bible study, it seemed the best they could do. Josie promised to call Hope right away and let Pamela know how that went but she didn't give Pamela Hope's information. That needed to be Hope's decision.

An hour later Josie was exhausted, mentally and emotionally. Her conversation with Hope had been difficult, at best. Hope didn't believe anything Pamela had to say and thought Josie was an idiot being taken in by a wild story. Josie could only say what Pamela had told her and agreed that they needed to talk to their dad before things went much further. Hope decided to go home the weekend after next. Josie decided to go home that weekend also, if Scott would let her leave at noon on Friday. Maybe if the three of them sat down and talked they could get the real story.

Josie didn't want to believe all of Pamela's story because it sure put her dad in a bad light. But the more she thought about her mother's version of what happened all those years ago, the more things just seemed to fit into place. Questions she hadn't really been conscious of seemed to have been answered. It felt true.

Josie placed one quick call to PJ at home. "PJ? I'm sorry to call you again but I wanted to let you know what's happening." After she briefed him on her two phone calls and the plans she and Hope had made, he prayed with her that God would lead them to the truth and help them all accept it, whatever it was.

It was too late to call Pamela back tonight and Josie was glad. I don't think I could handle one more thing today, she thought. Wish I could talk to Scott about this. As she got ready to take her shower she thought, yeah, like he's really going to want to hear more of my problems.

She lay awake a long time, her mind busy trying to put every piece together and come up with a complete picture. When she fell asleep it was to sleep fitfully, dreaming of her fragmented family.

Chapter 12

Scott looked up when Josie nearly stumbled into the shop.

"Hey, Josie! Been walking long?"

"What?"

"It's just a joke. Looked like you were having trouble with the basics of walking, etc. I was just giving you a bad time."

"Oh."

"You okay?" Scott laid down his hammer and walked over to Josie. "You look a wee bit tired?"

"Just a wee bit," Josie attempted a smile. "I know I slept for several hours last night but I feel like I ran a marathon instead." "Something happen?"

"You could say that. But I doubt we have the time this morning to go over the latest chapter in my totally messed up life."

"Let's take a few minutes and hit the highlights, okay?"

So, as briefly as she could, Josie told Scott about the phone calls to her mother and her sister. "I know we have to talk to Dad about this, but I am not looking forward to it. Hope doesn't believe Mom and I have no idea what I believe."

"Boy!" Scott said, "if it rains it pours, doesn't it?"

"I guess. Anyway, thanks for listening. But we'd better get to work, don't you think?"

They went over the first three tickets for the day and Josie loaded up on the supplies she'd need and left. It's good to have Scott to talk to again, but I wonder just what he's thinking about this family situation of mine. Sure, not the way to get a guy's attention, unless you want negative attention. And I don't. Even if he would consider me as more than a friend at some point, this is probably not going to advance my cause with him, she figured. Well, all I can do right now is go day by day. I have no idea how this will all work out. I guess it's up to God, now. Then she smiled. Guess it's always up to God, I just don't always realize it.

Throughout her day she vacillated between leaving it with God and taking it back and thinking it to death. She liked leaving it with God; that was a luxury she'd never before had. But old habits die hard and she was used to making her decisions and dealing with the results. Of course, she'd never dealt with anything this complex before.

I wonder how all of this would be hitting me if I hadn't become a Christian, she thought. I wouldn't have had PJ to help me, to talk to Mom, to advise me. And what about Jim and Barb? I'm sure they would still listen and be sympathetic. But I might not have been open to their counsel about the Lord. Not that I understand everything they say but I am learning, and they understand that it's all very new to me. I'm sure glad they're on my side.

SCOTT SHOOK HIS HEAD as Josie left. What a mess! That poor kid has more than she needs to deal with right now. Part of it she contributed to but the stuff with her parents sure wasn't her fault. Man, I cannot imagine what it would be like to have your mother leave, especially when you were that young. Mom has always been there for us kids. Guess we didn't realize how blessed we were and are. I've sure never had any reason to think she didn't care about me. It has to really be tough to grow up thinking your mother just left you and didn't even care enough to call or write.

And what about her dad? Even if he was wrong about why she left to take care of her mother, it had to be tough to try to raise two girls alone. Pretty lonely, too, I guess. After all, when you marry someone, you assume you'll be together, raise a family together, grow old together. Too bad he misunderstood things and made it worse.

BARB CALLED AROUND NOON to see how Josie was doing but she wasn't in yet. Scott told her that Josie had shared highlights with him.

"Yes. She's really having a rough time. All we can do is pray for her and be there for her," Barb said. "Just tell her I called to see how she's doing and to remind her I'm here if she needs me."

As Scott hung up the phone, he couldn't help but thank the Lord for the wonderful mother he had. Father too. We are truly blessed, he thought. I know I've never realized that, totally, before. Wonder about the others.

I bet Brenda has given it some thought since she's a mother herself. Poor Josie. She sure got cheated.

HIS THOUGHTS WERE DISRUPTED with Josie, herself, returning to the shop. He told her of Barb's call and then of how he was realizing how blessed he and his siblings were to have such wonderful parents.

"Yes, you are," Josie agreed. "I almost feel jealous of you all."

Scott nodded. "I know we've never truly appreciated them. I, for one, just took it for granted that parents were like them."

"You can't blame yourself; I think most kids are like that," she assured him. "I'm learning that things aren't always as they appear."

"It's gotta be strange to not know if what you've been told all your life is the way it really was."

"It's weird," she agreed. "It would never have occurred to me to doubt my Dad or to doubt anything he said. Now I just don't know."

"It must be hard to reconcile your feelings and questions when you love him so much."

"Hope is so mad at me for even considering that he didn't tell us the truth. She thinks I'm selling out to Mom and that Mom is obviously lying."

"She's older than you, isn't she?"

"Two years."

"Do you think she has some buried memories she hasn't ever faced, and this is shaking them loose?"

"I'd never thought about it, but I think that could be possible. Right after Mom left Hope told me that the folks were fighting about something. We didn't know what, but I guess we always figured it was the reason Mom left."

"Kind of scary, to have your mom leave when you were so young."

"It was. For a long time, we were afraid Dad would leave us, too. One of us would slip into his room at night to be sure he was still there. In the morning the first thing we did was to find him, so we knew he hadn't left us. We finally stopped checking so much but, deep inside, we were always afraid if he got mad at us, he'd leave."

"So, you were afraid to make a mistake?"

"Yeah. The first time I brought home a report card that had a 'c' on it I was terrified. I'd have happily endured a beating if I'd only known that he wouldn't either leave or send me away."

"What did he say?"

"About the 'c'? Said I could do better and that I should pay attention to the teacher and ask questions when I needed help."

"Pretty mild, considering how scared you were."

"I was so relieved that I started crying. He thought he'd been too harsh on me and pulled me onto his lap and just held me and told me how much he loved me." Josie smiled. "Then Hope got mad at me for being 'a cry baby.'"

"Was she jealous, do you think?"

"Maybe." Josie shrugged her shoulders. "Most of the time we got along pretty good. But once in a while she'd really get irritated with me and I learned to stay out of her way, then."

"I think all kids are that way. Sometimes my younger siblings drove me crazy, especially when I became a teenager. Brenda, being older, probably got irritated with all three of us." Scott smiled, remembering. "I know there were times when she really wanted to throttle me."

"Were you a pesky younger brother?"

"You could say that. Especially when she started dating. I was awful!"

"I'll bet you were!"

"Hey, don't be so quick to agree with me!"

"Just giving my honest opinion and observation."

"Oh, you are such a troublemaker," Scott joked. "I wish. . .

The ringing of the phone interrupted him. It was for Josie, so he handed it to her and then went over to his drafting table to give her some privacy. It's not mom, he thought. I'm sure she's never gotten a call before. Sure hope this isn't bad news of some sort. He glanced her way but she seemed okay, so he went back to his drawings.

Josie spoke for a few minutes then hung the phone up and came over to Scott. "That was Connie Adamson. She and Tim want me to know they aren't mad at me for presenting myself as a guy." She smiled. "I'm really glad. I liked them a lot and enjoyed myself when I ate with them a couple of Sundays ago."

"So, that's where you went instead of coming to our house?"

"Yes. They're in the Tuesday night Bible class."

"I don't know them well but have visited some with Tim. They seem very nice," Scott agreed. "What does he do, do you know?"

"I think he said he works on computers someplace. I know Connie is a nurse at a hospital."

"That would be Regional Hospital. It's the only one here but it's quite large as it services many smaller communities."

"You mean, they have to come all the way to Rapid City for their care?" Josie was astonished. "You'd think they would have something closer."

"Most of the smaller areas have hospitals and emergency rooms but send patients for more critical care to Regional. They get initial care in their own communities," Scott assured her. "That's better than having to be air lifted to Denver or Minneapolis."

"Yeah. I guess it is better. In Billings we have two hospitals, and I don't think Billings is any bigger than Rapid City."

THE PHONE RANG AGAIN, and Josie reached into the refrigerator for her lunch. She got a soda out of the machine and sat down to eat. When she was done, she took the job tickets Scott handed her and left. Scott was still on the phone, so she just waved.

Chapter 13

SATURDAY MORNING FOUND JOSIE awake just after the sun came up. *No fair,* she murmured. *This isn't even a workday. Why did I wake up this early?* Then she remembered. *Oh, yes. Today I will see Mom. What will I say to her? How will I know if she's telling me the truth? Maybe this isn't such a good idea.*

She sat on the side of the bed, wondering how to pass the time until 10:00 when she'd meet Pamela at Perkins. She'd gotten through the week pretty well by refusing to think about it. When she caught herself thinking or worrying about today's meeting, she just forced herself to think about the job she was on, what she was reading in her Bible, or something Scott said.

But now, this is the day. Good or bad, I'm going to see her. Oh, please, God, help me. I don't know what to do. I'm excited but scared. I want to see her but I'm afraid to see her. I want to hear about her family, but I know it will be painful for me. Oh, please help me.

Josie opened her Bible to John 15. She came to the fifth verse which concluded saying, "*. . .for without me ye can do nothing.*" *Boy, is that ever true,* she thought. She read on and found many references to loving one another and how much Jesus loves us. She saw where Jesus said that she had not chosen Him but that He had chosen her. *Wow. I'm sure I saw that before; this is my fourth time through this book. But I don't remember seeing it. Every time I read this book, I see something new.*

Josie read on for a couple more chapters. Then she sank to her knees by her bed. *Jesus, you know this is still pretty new to me. But I want to live like you want me to, but I don't do so good at it. Maybe I need more help* from you. Please help me today as I meet my mom. Please help me to know what is true, what I can believe. It's all so confusing. I keep trying to figure it out, but I just get more bewildered. I need your help. Thank you. Amen. Oh, yes, I forgot. Please help Hope. We're both scared and confused but at least I have you to help me. Thank you again. Amen.

JOSIE ENTERED PERKINS AT 9:30 to get a booth where she and Pamela could talk. If I'm here first I can watch for her. That'll be easier than walking in later and having to look for her. But when she opened the door a woman immediately rushed up to her, threw her arms around her and said, "Oh, Josie!! Oh, Josie! I can't believe you're really here."

"Mom?" Josie pulled back to get a look at her mother. "I can't believe you're here so early."

"I've been here for twenty minutes, hoping you'd get here early, too. I just couldn't wait."

The hostess found them a booth and gave them menus. When their waiter came ten minutes later the menus were untouched and the two women were still holding hands and talking. At about 11:30 they finally slowed down enough to order lunch, but they ate very little of it when it arrived.

Pamela showed Josie pictures of her younger children, Eric and Andrea, called Andi. Josie learned that Eric was ten and Andi was eight, they both played soccer, did well in school and had both committed their lives to the Lord Jesus.

"What about your husband?" Josie asked.

"Patrick teaches at the college there," Pamela said. "He also coaches soccer and teaches Sunday School."

"He sounds nice. How did you meet him?"

"At church. I was going through a bad time; I was missing you girls and Sam. I didn't know what to do. I showed up in his Sunday School class one Sunday and kept coming back. I got saved shortly thereafter and had so many questions."

Josie nodded, "I know."

"Yes. I was about where you're at now. Patrick was so knowledgeable and so kind. We started getting together after services to study the Bible and to answer my questions. We were just friends for two years while I was trying to get my life straightened out. After I got the divorce papers in the mail I really fell apart."

"I never thought about it. Is it okay for you to get married when you're divorced? They didn't kick you out of the church or anything?"

"I thought about that, too. Mostly, I felt like used merchandise that no one, not even God, would want. But we were allowed to marry, and I've been so grateful. I was so lonely, and I missed you girls so much."

"We sure missed you."

"Did you think I'd just abandoned you?"

"We knew you guys had fought about something, but we didn't know what. Then when you stopped sending cards and calling, we figured you just didn't care anymore."

"But I didn't stop sending cards, Sam just sent them back. When I called he wouldn't let me talk to you. Finally, he changed the phone number and had it unlisted. When I showed up there one time, he called the sheriff and had me thrown off the place before you girls got home from school. He went to court and got a restraining order against me. Here, I brought the copy I was served with."

As Josie read it, tears blurred her eyes. It was true. Wiping her tears away every couple of lines, she managed to read the entire thing. What a hateful document it was. And knowing it had kept her mother away from her for all these years just broke her heart.

"Josie. I'm so sorry. I shouldn't have brought it. Please don't cry."

Pamela moved over into the seat beside Josie and put her arms around her. "There, there. It's okay. Don't cry now."

Josie just leaned into her mother and cried all the harder. All the years she'd thought Pamela didn't care. All the times she'd asked her dad and he'd gotten angry. All the nights she'd cried herself to sleep, wanting her mother to come back.

Finally, she seemed to run out of tears, but her body still shook with sobs. Pamela just kept stroking her hair and face, soothing her. At last she seemed to be getting control; she wiped her eyes and blew her nose then smiled at Pamela. "I'm sorry, Mom. I didn't mean to cry."

"Oh, Josie. It's my fault. I shouldn't have brought that restraining order. I was just afraid you wouldn't believe me if I didn't."

"No, you were right to bring it. I don't know if I would have believed you or not. But seeing it was awful." Josie blew her nose again.

"I just can't believe Dad lied to us all those years."

"Josie, your dad is a good man. He was just so insecure about me. For some reason he thought I'd lowered myself to marry him and he was desperately afraid that I wouldn't stay. When I came home to see my mom, he just couldn't believe I was telling the truth."

"Yeah, but when you kept trying to come back, he should have realized that he hadn't lost you," Josie insisted.

"Yes. You'd think. But he decided I'd betrayed him and had an affair with Dylan, so I'd become damaged goods, as he put it, and he didn't want me back."

"Mom, he's been so lonely." Pictures of Sam, always alone or with them, filled Josie's mind. As a child she hadn't thought about it, of course. But now, looking back, she knew he'd been terribly lonely.

"I'm sure. I'd hoped, once he divorced me, that he'd find someone. Then you girls would have had a mom, a woman to help you."

"I don't ever remember him going out with anyone. He was always there for us. He really tried to be both dad and mom to us. But it was hard. When Aunt Helen came to town, it helped a lot. We girls had so many questions. She was very patient and loving with us."

"Aunt Helen? Hmm. I don't remember her." Pamela looked puzzled. "Are you sure she was your aunt?"

"Yes. Dad said she was his sister."

"Josie, your dad didn't have any siblings. He was an only child."

"Well, I dunno. He said she was his sister. We girls loved her. She was a real blessing to us, whoever she was."

"You said she was a blessing. Is she no longer around there?"

"She died," Josie said. "She was killed by a drunk driver."

"Oh, that's too bad," Pamela said. "I'm sure that was very hard for you girls."

"Yes. At least by then we were both through our teen years. I don't know what we'd have done without her then." Josie smiled. "She wasn't afraid of Dad, either. She really got after him if she thought he wasn't doing something right by us girls."

"I'm glad someone was on your side—a woman. Girls need a woman to help them and guide them through those turbulent years."

Pamela looked at her watch. "Oh, my dear, I need to go. We already had dinner plans before I spoke with you and I didn't cancel them. I was sure we'd be talked out long before now."

Josie smiled. "I don't know if we could ever get talked out, Mom. It seems like the more we talk the more questions I have."

Pamela stood up and Josie slid out of the booth. They stopped at the cashier and Pamela paid their tickets. As they left, both with teary, red eyes, they held hands, both reluctant to let go.

"Josie, it's an answer to prayer to get to see you today. I'd begun to think it wouldn't ever happen."

"Me too. Of course, I was angry at you and convinced myself I didn't care if I ever saw you again or not." Josie blew her nose. "What a liar!"

Josie told Pamela that she was going home the next weekend to see Hope and Sam. Promising to let her know how that went as soon as she was back in town, Josie climbed into her truck. Then she climbed back down to give Pamela one more hug before they went their separate ways.

She had her mother back! Actually, in one way, she'd never lost her. Pamela had never stopped loving her; she hadn't walked away from them; she had tried to stay in contact. That was such a comforting thought that it almost wiped out the heart break of knowing Sam had intentionally lied to her and Hope and prevented their mother from being a part of their lives. Almost.

THE NEXT WEEK PASSED slowly but at last it was Friday noon. Josie drove into the shop yard and unloaded her tools and supplies. Scott smiled at her and said, "so, you're deserting me now, huh?"

"Yup. I'm running away from home. Well, actually, I'm running away to home this time."

"I sure hope your trip goes well, Josie. I'll be praying for you and I know my family is also."

"Thanks. I appreciate it. I need all the prayer I can get."

"Let's pray before you go, okay?" Scott reached for Josie's hands then offered a simple prayer asking God to give Josie a safe trip and to bless her efforts to find the truth and to unite her family. Then Josie was on her way. Scared, maybe terrified, but on her way.

Chapter 14

"Josie! This is the craziest thing I've ever heard!" Hope yelled. "No way did Dad lie to us about her. Why would he?"

"I know it's hard, Hope but try to. . ."

"Try to what? Believe her lies?"

"Hope, I do believe she's telling the truth," Josie said, pleading with her sister. "Won't you let me tell you the whole thing? Please."

"No. I refuse to listen to her wild stories. What does Dad say about this?"

"I haven't talked to him about it since I got home. I tried asking him about some of it on the phone, but he just got mad."

"See? If it was true, Dad would have admitted it."

It was Saturday morning and the girls had met in a parking lot in Billings, wanting to talk together before they met with their dad. Now Hope opened the door to Josie's truck and got out. "I'm going home. I've been wanting to come back to visit and I'm going to spend as much time as I can with Dad." She slammed the door and walked to her car.

Josie just sat, thinking. This didn't go too well, Lord. What do I do now? After a few minutes she started up her truck and headed for home down the familiar streets. She'd gotten in about 8:30 the night before, surprising her dad. He'd been glad to see her, and they'd talked quite late into the night.

Josie had told him her problems with her identity had worked out and everyone was treating her well. Then she'd mentioned that she was going to church and Sam hit the roof. Josie didn't press it any further, not wanting to fight with her dad. They'd found safer subjects and enjoyed the company and the conversation, as her dad was fond of saying.

For Josie it had been bittersweet; knowing that by today there could be a chasm between them that might never be bridged. When she was with him, she couldn't imagine that he could have lied to them and driven their mother out of their lives. Then she'd remember Pamela and what she'd said, and her emotions were all twisted up again.

Now she turned into the driveway and braced herself for battle as she got out of her truck and walked toward the house. Hope's car was there so Josie figured she was walking into an angry beehive.

"Josie? What's this garbage your sister is talking about?" Sam demanded as she entered. Shutting the door behind her, Josie took a deep breath and walked over to her dad.

"I've met with Mom and heard her side of the story. Hope and I just want to know the truth," Josie said gently. "Dad, we love you, but we need to know what really happened with Mom."

"I told you what happened. She left and didn't come back," Sam said angrily. "What else is there to tell?"

"What about her wanting to come home and you refusing her?" Josie asked. "What about you divorcing her?"

"She didn't ever want to come back. I divorced her to get her out of my life for good," he insisted.

"And out of ours?"

"Yes. And out of yours. She didn't want you, so why not?"

"What about getting a restraining order against her because she did show up here, wanting to see Hope and me?"

"Dad?" Hope looked at her dad, begging him to deny what Josie had just said. "Is it true?"

"Of course not. Why would I want to keep her from seeing you girls?"

"Dad. I read the restraining order," Josie said softly.

"Josie! You read it? Why didn't you tell me?" Hope asked.

"You wouldn't let me," Josie explained. "I wouldn't have believed it but Mom brought her copy when I met with her last week."

"Dad?" Hope asked.

"Oh, all right! By the time she came prowling around here she'd been gone so long I figured you girls were better off without her," he admitted. "And you were!"

Both girls looked at him, incredulously. Josie looked at Hope and saw fear in her sister's eyes.

"It's okay, Hope," she reassured her sister.

"Dad. What about the letters and cards Mom sent that you wouldn't let us have?"

"You know, Josie, that your mother sent cards the first couple of years and then just stopped. I can't do anything about that." With that, Sam rose to his feet and stomped out of the room. "I'm not going to sit here and listen to this garbage. I'm your dad, I'm the one that was here for you for all of these years. If that's not good enough, then so be it." He stopped in the doorway and said, "You two need to get back to where you belong.

I don't want you here when I get back."

JOSIE GRABBED THE OVERNIGHT bag she'd brought and put it in her truck. Hope did the same, so they were both outside within five minutes of Sam's tirade. He was no where to be seen. Josie turned to Hope. "You going to head back right away?"

"I'd like to talk someplace, if we can," Hope said. "I wish I'd listened to you earlier."

"It's a lot to absorb, Hope. I know. I've been trying to for almost two weeks."

"It's just hard for me to believe that Dad would do that to us," Hope stated. "He was always there for us. I can't make the two things go together."

"Hope, I have something for you. Mom gave me the letters and cards she'd sent to us that were refused and returned to her. She kept them; they haven't even been opened. She thought that someday we might want them."

"You brought mine?"

Josie opened the bag she had thrown on the passenger seat. Finding a large envelope with Hope's name on it, she handed it to her. Hope just looked at her. "Really? These are all mine?"

Josie nodded. "Want to go somewhere to read them?"

"I'd like to go somewhere and talk and read them. Did you get yours?" Hope looked like someone had punched her in the stomach. Josie could identify with that sick feeling; she'd been dealing with it since she'd first spoken with Pamela. She moved closer to her sister and put an arm around her.

"Yes. But I haven't read them. I thought we might want to do it together."

They agreed on a small park that was usually pretty quiet, stopped by a drive in to pick up drinks and parked near their old favorite tree. Josie always carried a blanket, so they put that on the grass and settled in. Hope put her cards and letters in order by the cancellation date stamped on them.

Watching her, Josie could see that Hope's hands were trembling.

"Okay. Here's the first one." As Hope opened and read her first card, Josie got the last of hers in order and opened the first one. These had been sent within a month of their mother's departure.

"Hope? Mom sent these right away. We obviously didn't get them. I remember getting birthday and Christmas cards but nothing in between."

"That's what I was thinking, too," Hope agreed. "It looks like he started off sending them back. I wonder why he went ahead and gave us the other cards?"

"I wonder if Mom talked him into it after he sent these first things back," Josie murmured, her mind more occupied with the words her mother had written in this note to her.

"Could be. Maybe you can ask her," Hope responded. "I'm so glad to know she did send us stuff. She didn't just forget us like Dad said."

Josie agreed. It seemed so important right now to know that Pamela hadn't just given up on them.

The girls were busy for over an hour reading words their mother had lovingly written to them so many years ago, occasionally sharing something with the other but mostly reading and crying a bit.

Hope finally said, "I guess it really is true, isn't it? Dad did lie to us all those years and he didn't give us what she sent. What an awful thing to do to your kids."

"Yes. I know. I've thought about it a lot. Scott's mother said I should remember that he was probably doing what he thought was the best for all of us."

"Mostly for himself, it looks like." Hope stood up, angrily, and started pacing. "Seems like what was best for us would have been to be raised by our mother."

"Mom says he always felt like she lowered herself by marrying him, so he was always afraid she'd leave. Maybe he'd worried about it so much that when she left to take care of her mother, he just figured that his fears had come true."

"Why would he think she was too good for him?" Hope asked.

"Mom said it always bothered him that she had a college degree and he didn't. She said she didn't think anything of it, that Dad was so good at what he did she was a bit intimidated by him. But it bugged Dad," Josie explained.

"That's goofy!" stated Hope. "Dad's the best at what he does."

"We know that but maybe he doesn't really believe it."

"That's sad."

By the time the girls had read and talked and cried and read some more, it was too late for either of them to start out on their return trips. They decided to pool their money and rent a motel room and then start out early Sunday morning.

"Hope! I just remembered something else to tell you. "Mom remarried and she has a boy, Eric, who is ten and a girl, Andrea—who goes by Andi-who is eight."

"We have a brother? And another sister?" Hope seemed pleased. "What are they like?"

"I haven't met them yet," Josie explained. "All I know is that they both play soccer."

As GIRLS WILL DO, they talked far into the night. Although they didn't re-solve anything about their current situation, they did regain the closeness both had missed since they'd gone their separate ways. Hope agreed to talk to Pamela on the phone and she and Josie agreed to stay in closer touch with each other. Promising to stay close and to try to work things out between them and their parents, they finally fell asleep.

Sunday morning after a quick bite at a fast food place, they hugged good-bye and each headed out for where they now called home.

Josie was drained. She'd failed with her dad. At least Hope is speaking to me, she thought. I never did tell her about my stupid adventure going to Rapid City. In fact, she realized, I never did even tell her what I'm doing there. We just didn't have time and it didn't seem important.

Chapter 15

Josie got to work a bit early Monday morning. *Just in case Scott is really backed up by my leaving early Friday,* she thought. *He's been so good to me through all of this.*

"Hey, boss man, ready to work?" she greeted him when she walked in.

"Josie! Good to see you made it back okay. How'd it go? Pretty tough?"

"Well, it wasn't a walk in the park, that's for sure," Josie said lightly.

"Your dad admit anything?" Scott asked, hoping he wasn't getting too nosy. But they'd talked about it all so much he felt Josie wanted him to know.

"Yes. And no," Josie hesitated. "He did finally admit he divorced her but nothing else."

"And your sister?"

"At first she was just mad at me. But giving her Mom's letters did it for her. I don't know what it will take to get things right between us and Dad, though."

"But you're going to try?"

"I guess so. I really don't know where to go with this right now. I want to call Mom and give her Hope's phone number so they can talk. Beyond that, I'm not sure. Think I need to talk to PJ again."

"Probably not a bad idea," Scott agreed. "He has a different perspective on things that can be helpful."

"I hope he doesn't get sick of me bugging him," Josie said. "I have really been a pain to him."

"I don't think he would look at it that way. He's trained in counseling so it's not like he's in over his head. Besides, he's got God giving him directions and insights and such so he's a head above any other counselor."

"But other counselors get paid for listening to other people's problems," Josie said. "I've wondered if I should be offering to pay PJ. I just haven't known how to ask."

"PJ does get paid," Scott asserted. "Both in the salary he receives but also in the blessings of the Lord. God rewards those who serve him and obey him, you know. I'm certain he would not accept any kind of payment from you. This is all part of his calling."

"Okay. If you say so. Guess I'll call him later and see if he has time for me," Josie agreed. "But now I'm sure you have work for me to do."

"I do, indeed," Scott said, laughing. "And since I'm the original slave driver I'd better put you to work." He handed her a pile of tickets. "No one is an emergency so look through these and pick where you want to start," he offered.

Josie picked a couple that she thought would be in the same neighborhood, verified it with Scott, loaded her tools and supplies back into her truck and left. I'm really lucky to have such a good job and boss, she thought. A month ago, I'd have questioned my still being here if Scott found out about me. But here I am, still employed. And Scott still looks good, really good, to me. Better, actually, than before. I missed him this weekend.

Knock it off! She admonished herself. Stop talking like a silly schoolgirl. You're a 24-year-old woman! Grow up!

But her mind drifted back to Scott Mayforth. He is a fine man; yes indeed, he is. Ah, yes. But, is he already spoken for? No signs of a girl friend but that's not proof. I'll have to ask him, just to be sure.

She grinned. This isn't getting better. If anything, it's getting worse. I do think the time has come and I have fallen for a guy! Me! Josie!

Scott watched Josie leave with mixed emotions. She had obviously had a difficult weekend and he wanted to be as supportive and helpful as he could without butting in where he wasn't wanted; but he also really wanted to know what was happening. She didn't say how she left things with her dad, he thought. But it didn't sound good. She's always been very close to him and learning that he wasn't truthful with her and her sister was obviously difficult for her. I wonder if talking to my folks would help? Well, Mom did call the other day to remind Josie that they're available. So, what do I do to be helpful but not in the way?

A customer walked in, a rare occurrence, and Scott turned to help him. The man was lost and looking for someone on a different street. Scott walked out with him and pointed out the way. As he returned to his work, he was reminded that sometimes just responding to a simple spoken need was very helpful. Encouraged, he shot his eyes Heaven ward. Thanks, Father. I can help by just doing what's needed as this proceeds.

That his mind was somewhat set at ease does not mean that Josie was far from his thoughts. Overriding his concerns for her problems was the awareness that this girl was really getting under his skin. Smiling ruefully he acknowledged being more interested in her than in any other girl he'd ever known.

She's a tough little cookie, he said to himself. But I think that outer shell hides a gentle soul. Even as a guy she couldn't totally camouflage her softness, her caring and her warmth. That was partly what kept bugging me, that didn't seem to go with the outer package, that I couldn't put my finger on.

What a dolt! I couldn't distinguish a girl from a guy? You'd think that in 28 years I would at least have learned how to do that. Shaking his head, he picked up his tape measure to check his marks before he started cutting wood. Measure twice, cut once he reminded himself. Dad must have told me that a thousand times. Bet he didn't think I'd ever learn. He grinned. I was lucky to have such a dad; some would have given up on me by about the third year, but Dad held firm. Kept saying he knew I could do it. Wonder if he ever felt like a liar?

His mind drifted back to Josie. I'm so glad she became a Christian but that's what started all of this mess, knowing she had to get out of the lie she was living. No, actually, all of this stuff with her family was unrelated to that; it just all hit at the same time. Sure hope PJ can keep helping her with all of her family problems. Wonder what her folks are like? It's easy to get a picture in your mind that might not be even close to the real thing.

Wonder if her dad would give her away? Whoa! Where did that come from? Who said anything about a wedding? Shaken, Scott walked over and got a soda from the machine. I haven't even gone out with her; how can I be thinking about marrying her?

So lost in his thoughts was he that when she returned, she had to slam the door twice to get his attention.

"What is it you're so fond of saying? Earth to Scott! Earth to Scott!"

Startled, he turned toward the door. "Oh, hi, Josie. I didn't hear you come in! You're back early, aren't you?"

"Early for what? It's a quarter past noon."

"Oh, yeah. Sorry. Guess I was daydreaming," Scott stammered.

"What's the matter with you? You okay?" Josie's smile disappeared and a look of concern replaced it. "Did something happen?"

"Naw. I'm fine. My mind was just somewhere else."

"Obviously. Where? If you don't mind my asking?"

"Well, actually, I was thinking about you."

"Me? What, the mess I've made of everything?"

"I wouldn't say that. None of the problems with your family are your fault," Scott defended her.

"Well, what then?"

Taking a deep breath, Scott turned so he wasn't quite facing Josie and asked, "Do you think you'd ever like to go out with me?"

"What? Speak up! Are you asking me for a date?" Josie laughed.

"Really, now?"

"Not a good idea?" he questioned, more disappointed than he'd thought he could be.

"You mean you're serious?" she demanded.

"Yeah. I thought we might try it, if you're game." Maybe there's still hope?

"Hmm. I suppose we might. Guess that answers my question." She laughed. "What did you have in mind?"

"What question?"

"Whether or not you had a girl friend." Josie said, feeling like she was blushing. For goodness sake!

"Nope. Not yet, anyway." He grinned. Maybe he could change that soon.

"Okay. Well what about this date?" Josie hoped she sounded casual enough. Her heart was beating like a tom-tom drum.

"Well, we talked about going down to the Park for a play. Want to try that?"

"What Park?" What was he talking about?

"Custer State Park. Don't you remember? We were going to go through the Park and then go to the Playhouse for a musical," Scott reminded her.

"Oh, that's right. That's what Terry was talking about, right?"

"Yeah." She doesn't sound very interested. Now what?

"Well, he'll want to go, won't he?"

"What he wants and what he gets are two different things. He can go another time," Scott stated. "I think the Music Man is playing now. Want to go Saturday?"

So, Scott picked Josie up just after lunch on Saturday and they headed out for the State Park. Josie hadn't been in this part of the Black Hills and thoroughly enjoyed the beautiful scenery. As they came closer to the Park the road seemed to be a bit curvier but slowing down allowed them to see more of the natural beauty. When they arrived at the entrance, the attendant saw Scott's Park Permit and just waved them through. But Scott stopped to ask a question and the attendant came to the car.

"Good afternoon, sir."

"Good afternoon. I was just wondering if the Wild Life Loop is the best drive right now to see the buffalo or if they've wandered off to another area?"

"No, that's a good plan today. They're not moving around a lot because of the heat."

"Thank you. Hope you have a great rest of the day," Scott said as he drove on. "You never know for sure what you'll see on any given day. Sometimes you'll only spot a few buffalo from the road and other times you have to wait to let a herd of them cross the road."

"Really? This should be way cool." Josie was twisting around in her seat trying to look out in every direction. "Oh, look! What's that?"

"Where?"

"Over there, by that tree." She pointed out her window.

"Well, I'm not sure, Josie, but it looks like a log to me,"

"Oh, Scott!"

"Sorry, Josie. I'm sure we'll see some animals soon." Scott laughed. "I'm not really laughing at you. Us kids used to always see stuff and we about drove our folks crazy. Most of the time there was nothing there."

"Right." Josie was embarrassed. "But that's something over there, right?"

As Scott quickly stopped the car, he smiled at her. "Yup. That's definitely something."

"Well, what is it? A deer?"

"It's an elk. Isn't he beautiful?"

"Oh, I wish I'd brought my camera from home. I was going to get some more of my stuff but didn't really get a chance."

"I have a small one in the glove compartment if you want to use it," Scott offered. "But, truly, the best pictures are on the post cards at the various businesses."

"Okay. That sounds like a good idea. I'd like to send a couple to Hope. I'm trying to talk her into moving down here. We could get an apartment and she could go to school here."

"So, you want to use the wildlife in the Park as bait?"

"Sure. Whatever works."

"Sounds like a plan." But I hope you're not real set on sharing an apartment with your sister. I have a much better idea.

They drove slowly through the Park and were lucky enough to see several white tail deer, some big horn sheep, a few prairie dogs and many buffalo. When they crested the hill and the herd was just before them, Josie gasped. "Oh, Scott! They're so big!"

"That they are," he agreed. "And they are the boss. They aren't violent but if you try to hurry them or mess with them in any way, they can do a lot of damage."

"I wouldn't think of it," Josie said promptly. "I never argue with something that's that much bigger than me."

"Smart girl."

They stopped at Sylvan Lake and walked around it. "It's so peaceful and pretty here," Josie breathed.

"I like to come here. Some time when we have more time we'll see if they still rent boats. But I think that soon we need to start meandering towards our supper."

"Is it that late, already?" Josie looked at her watch. "Why, it's past five! I can't believe we've been here this long."

"Time in the Park always passes quickly for me. I love to come here and usually get down here at least a couple times a month, except in the winter."

"Why not the winter?"

"I come down, just not quite as often. Mostly because there's usually so much going on at work, at church, I like to go skiing, and that type of thing. It's beautiful here in the winter, though. I'll make sure we get down so you can see."

"You're sure making a lot of plans for 'us', aren't you?" Josie asked with a grin. "Something here you want to tell me, boss?"

Scott feigned innocence. "Whatever do you mean, ma'am?"

"You know!"

"Say, Josie, I think we should be getting down to Blue Bell Lodge. We have reservations but if they're really busy we could still have to wait some. The play is at 8:00 but we need to be there by 7:30." Scott reached for her elbow and gently directed her towards his car.

Josie giggled. "Boy, one would think you were trying to change the subject or something."

"Who, me?" Scott laughed as he closed her door and went around to his. "I just want to be sure we get our dinner. I'm a growing boy and I'm getting hungry."

"I sure hope you're NOT a growing boy!" Josie made motions with her hands to indicate growing outward rather than upward. "I've never been overly fond of men with pot bellies."

"Thanks for the warning."

They chatted amiably all through dinner and on the drive to the Playhouse. When they were seated, Scott showed her how all of the actors and actresses as well as other employees of the Playhouse were all in the playbill. Not everyone in the book would be in the musical they were seeing tonight but would have already participated in a production or would be in one yet to come. "Some, if you'll notice, have been coming to be a part of this for years and years." He showed her someone who, according to the book, was there for their 18th season.

"Wow. That's a lot of commitment, isn't it?" Josie was impressed.

The music started and they settled back to enjoy the production. On their way back to Rapid City they talked about the musical, comparing it to the movie. "I just always think that Winthrop has to be Ronnie Howard," Josie stated. "But I do think this little boy did a good job."

"I enjoy every play they do. We'll have to check and see what's still left. I did know but cannot remember." Scott reached over and took Josie's hand. It felt right, to both of them.

Chapter 16

Josie woke up Sunday morning with a smile on her face. She could feel it. Yesterday with Scott had been so good. She'd loved the Park, the Playhouse, and the dinner; but the best of all had been being with Scott.

We're just on the same wavelength, she thought. We were truly comfortable with each other. In a good way. I didn't feel all nervous like you usually would on a first date. I don't think Scott did, either.

She got up and walked to the bathroom and looked in the mirror to see the smile she knew was there. Yup. It's still there. Goofy girl! It was just one date. She reached her hand up to wipe the smile away, but it just came back. Oh, well.

She dressed for church more carefully than usual. Now that she could wear her real clothes it was a lot more fun getting dressed to go out. She'd opted to stay with the same work clothes other than switching to short sleeves. But church was another matter. Hmm. This blue skirt looks good with this paisley blouse I got downtown last week. As she combed her mid length hair back and fastened it with combs she debated on earrings. Ah, yes. These pearls will be perfect.

She picked up her Bible and started out the door. Oops. Guess I should get breakfast first. Laying her Bible down on the dresser, she grabbed her key, locked her room, and scooted down the steps. On Sundays Mrs. Stewart usually laid out a fine buffet and today was no exception. Josie filled her plate at the sideboard and sat down at the table to eat.

The Rapid City Journal was in the middle of the table, so she grabbed a section to peruse while she ate. It wasn't a very good habit, she knew, but when you're eating alone, reading is rather nice. She skimmed over the paper, stopping to read an article here and there, while she ate her waffle, fruit, scrambled eggs and drank her orange juice. Taking her dishes to the kitchen, she thanked her landlady for the breakfast and hurried upstairs.

When she arrived at the church, she realized she was still a little early as there weren't many cars. She opened her Bible to the New Testament and began to read. PJ and Scott had both told her she might want to read the four gospels now that she was pretty familiar with John.

Whoa! Matthew started with a lot of genealogy! Wonder if it's okay to skip this part? Oh, here it starts talking about the birth of Jesus. She read on and learned more in those few minutes about the first Christmas than she'd ever heard in her whole 24 years of life. Then the wise men came. Hmm. She'd always heard there were three, but Matthew didn't say how many. Wonder why?

Boy, that Herod was a bad character, killing all those babies! That's awful! Those poor families. At least they got Jesus away, so He was safe.

What a terrible way to live, running for your life.

She startled as someone knocked on her window. She looked up to see Scott's smiling face. Gathering up her Bible and keys, she accompanied Scott into the church. She was going with Scott to his class for her first time in Sunday School.

"You'll like it, Josie," he promised. "Everyone is about our age and the teacher is the youth pastor here." As they went, he introduced her to those they came across, everyone going to their own classes.

"I always thought Sunday school was for little kids," Josie admitted. "I had no idea that adults went."

"We all have much to learn and this is a good way to do it," Scott explained. "I started Sunday school when I was four, I think, and have only missed a handful of Sundays since."

The class was studying the book of Mark, which Josie hadn't read yet. But the teacher was very knowledgeable, and everyone got into the discussions. It was a lively time and Josie enjoyed it even if she didn't always understand everything they talked about. Better switch to Mark for my reading, she decided. I know some of this, from John, but there's sure a lot that's new to me.

Church followed the Sunday School hour and, as always, Josie hung on PJ's words. This is amazing, she thought. I can't believe I got this old without knowing any of this stuff. The Bible studies on Tuesday nights are definitely helpful but I've got a long way to go.

When they stood to sing the final hymn, Josie was pleased that it was one they'd sung before, so it was a little familiar to her. Scott's baritone voice blended nicely with her soprano and she really enjoyed the song.

Outside, Connie and Tim Adamson came over and greeted Josie.

"Wow. You really are a girl!" Connie said. "Cool!"

"Oh, hi, you guys," Josie responded, still a little uneasy with them.

"We won't keep you, looks like you're busy," Connie said with a smile and a wink. "But we want you to know that we truly don't hold it against you for pretending to be a guy. We enjoyed your company and would like to see you again."

"That's very nice of both of you," Josie said. "Thank you so much. It means a lot to me." Wow. They are incredible. They really mean it.

Tim smiled. "I have to say I'm very impressed that you can hold down that kind of a job, for Mr. Picky here."

"Hey! Don't be maligning my character," Scott protested.

"Actually, Josie, I was impressed when I thought you were a guy. I'm even more impressed now. Scott's quite a taskmaster. You must be very good at what you do." Tim punched Scott in the arm as he grinned at Josie.

Connie stepped in. "Okay, you guys. Cut it out."

Josie laughed. "I'm beginning to think it's a guy thing. I grew up with one sister, so we missed out on all of this testosterone. How DO you live with it?"

"You're right. It is a guy thing. I grew up with a couple of brothers so I'm kind of used to it. But once in a while I just have to send Tim out with the guys to bowl or play softball or whatever. Gets to be too much for me to handle." Connie was grinning at her husband.

Tim feigned embarrassment. "Oh, come on, honey, don't be telling that kind of stuff around."

Laughing, Tim took Connie's hand and started pulling her toward their car. "Hey, we'll have to get together with both of you soon."

Nodding and laughing, Josie and Scott walked to her truck. "Want to leave it here and ride over to the folks' with me? Scott asked.

"Why don't I drive over. Then I can leave when I need to. I want to try to call Mom later," Josie suggested.

"No. Ride with me, please?" he said. "I'll bring you back here the second you're ready to leave."

"Okay. I'm really looking forward to seeing your folks. They've sure been nice to me."

"You're not that hard to be nice to, you know?" Scott took her hand and led her to his car. As he helped her in he couldn't help but notice how feminine and pretty she looked. How could she do that? Work in a physically demanding job all week but be such a delicate flower now. He was still shaking his head when he got into the car.

"No, what?" Josie asked.

"Huh?"

"You were shaking your head 'no' when you got in."

"Oh, just amazed at how pretty and dainty you look today and yet how strong you are and how well you do your job throughout the week. I just don't understand how you do it."

Josie smiled. This is good. He does notice that I'm a gal and I think he likes what he sees. It's a start anyway.

Scott's thoughts were definitely on the girl in the car with him and he nearly missed the turn to his parents' street. He recovered without Josie noticing, he hoped. Then he realized that he'd actually turned on the wrong street after all. He took a right at the next corner and at the one after that.

"Scott? I'm lost. Where are we?'

"Don't you recognize this street?" he said, seriously.

"No. But I've only been there from the church a couple of times so I'm sure I just don't remember right."

He laughed. "Well, actually, I turned on the wrong street and now I'm trying to get to where we're supposed to be."

"You missed the street to your own home? How long did you live there?"

"22 years. But who's counting?"

"How'd you happen to miss your turn," Josie asked seriously.

Scott laughed. "I'm not sure I should tell you."

"Why?"

"Because I was thinking about you and that's why I messed up."

Josie laughed. "Good." The smile returned to her face.

They pulled up at the curb and Scott turned the car off. Getting out he went to Josie's side to open the door and help her out.

"Wow. A real gentleman," she commented, smiling. "I like this."

The front door opened and Jim Mayforth stepped out onto the porch. "Hi, you two," he greeted them. "Josie, it's good to see you again."

"Only her? Not good to see me," Scott pouted.

Jim laughed and opened the door for them all to enter. Scott followed Josie in and greeted the rest of his family. Barb came out of the kitchen to greet Josie. "Hello, Josie dear. It's good to see you. We missed seeing you last weekend. Scott says you went home."

"Yes, thank you Mrs. Mayforth. But it's good to be back. Home wasn't as friendly as it used to be," Josie said wryly.

"Want to talk about it? Why don't you come out to the kitchen with me? I just have a couple of things to do and then we can eat."

"Is there anything I can do," Josie offered, following Barb out.

"I think I have things pretty well ready to go but need to add the dressing to the salad and get the biscuits out of the oven. And, Josie," she looked directly at her guest, "Please call me Barb. Mrs. Mayforth was my mother-in-law and I loved her dearly. But that's who I look around for when someone uses that name."

"Thank you, if you're sure," Josie agreed.

"So, was your trip home very difficult?" Barb asked. As Josie started to respond Scott came into the kitchen.

"Are we about ready to eat? I'm starved."

"Scott, take this salad with you to the table and ask everyone to be seated. I just have to get the biscuits and Josie and I will be right in."

The dinner conversation was lively with everyone having an opinion on the sermon context. PJ had spoken about the Holy Spirit and how He works in our lives. It was all very new to Josie, of course, and she listened raptly both to his sermon and the table conversation.

When dinner was finished and the dishes loaded into the dishwasher, Barb again looked at Josie. "Josie, would you like to take a walk in my flower gardens? I thought we could talk there, if you like."

"I'd love to Mrs. May. . . er Barb."

As they walked outside through the patio and into the lovely back yard, surrounded with flowers, Josie oohed an aahed over the beauty.

Barb told her the kinds of flowers when she asked, and they just strolled for a few minutes. Then Barb brought her back to the topic at hand. "Was the weekend quite awful for you, dear, or did it go fairly well? We have prayed for you daily since you explained the situation."

"Well, my Dad did finally admit that he'd divorced Mom but just got very angry about everything else. I think if we could have talked longer, we might have gotten a bit further but he literally ordered us out of the house."

"Oh, my. That's too bad. How did it go with your sister?"

"Hope was extremely angry with me in the beginning as she couldn't believe Dad would have lied so she assumed Mom was. But when I gave her all the letters and cards Mom had sent to her that Dad refused and had returned, she saw the whole picture. She is very upset with Dad, as am I, but she just ate up the letters from Mom. We had always been told that Mom left us with no backward glance. To learn that she'd come back to see us and been ordered off the property and that Dad had even gotten a restraining order, well, that was astounding. We had no idea."

"I'm sure that, as traumatic as all of this is, it's still good for you girls to learn that your mother didn't just walk away and never think of you again."

"Yes. It made a big difference to both of us. I truly think we see ourselves as people with more value now. That's kind of goofy, I guess."

"Not at all. And it's good to have a better self image. God made us in His image, so we're not junk although the enemy likes for us to think we are." Barb put an arm around Josie's shoulders. "I know this must be hard, Josie. But I'm sure our heavenly Father will help you walk through the rest of it, step by step."

"You have no idea how comforting that is to me. I'm not used to the idea of having God on my side. It's very nice. I'm realizing it's a good thing, too, because He seems to be the only one who actually knows what's going on and the truth about the past."

They were still talking when Scott came out the back door. "Hey, Josie, you two finished with your girl talk?"

"Maybe. Who wants to know?" she asked sassily while smiling sweetly.

Barb laughed. "Hmm. I think Scott may have met his match." She gave Josie a quick hug and went back inside the house. "She's all yours," she said quietly to Scott as she passed him.

"I hope," he replied, just as quietly and walked over to Josie. "Hi," he said, reaching for her hand. "I missed you."

"Me, too."

"I hope you don't think I'm rushing you, Josie, but I think I started caring for your wit and kind ways long before I knew you were a girl. Then I just fell in love with the whole package. I feel as though I've known and loved you for ages, even though it hasn't been that long. Am I pushing?"

"No, I don't think so."

"But you're not sure?"

"There is just so much going on right now. I don't want to misinterpret my gratitude for your friendship and understanding. I think I'm falling in love with you, too. I just want to be sure."

Scott gently pulled Josie toward him, kissing her lightly on the lips, then just folding her into his embrace. Finally. He felt complete, content.

" I could get used to this," he said softly. "Indeed, I could get used to this."

"Hmm."

"What does that mean?"

"Me, too," Josie murmured. "Me, too."

They just stood like that for a couple of minutes, both content. "Josie, I feel like I've come home, like this is where I was meant to be."

She nodded her head. "Hmm." It felt like home to her, also. A nice loving home.

"Josie?"

"Hmm?"

"I think I love you."

"Me, too."

"Josie? I've never known you to say so little. Is there a problem?"

"Nope. I just feel so loved and safe; I never knew it could be like this."

"I'm glad."

"Josie?"

"Hmm."

"Will you marry me?"

That got her attention. She pulled back from his embrace and looked him in the eye. "Are you serious?"

"Yes. Not a good idea?"

"Oh, it's a very good idea. But I'm not sure if it's a smart idea."

"Why?"

"Scott, I'm not really sure who I am right now. I'm trying to figure out if I still have a Dad. I have a stepfather and sister and brother I haven't even met. A mother I've seen once since I was seven. I'm a big question mark. You might want to wait and see what you'd actually be getting before you decide to marry me."

"I'm not marrying your family. I'm marrying you," Scott insisted.

"My guess is that it may not always work out that way," Josie responded. "Who my family members are would impact our life together just as much as who your family is. The only thing is, I know what I'd be getting for in-laws. You don't."

"Okay. We could wait a couple of months."

Josie laughed. "You dear, dear man."

"Me?"

"Scott. I do love you. I think I started falling in love with you the first day we met. But I don't think I'm in any shape to promise myself to anyone. I have too much to sort out. Can you understand that?"

Pulling her back into his arms, Scott kissed the top of her head. "Josie, I'm sure you're right, that you have a lot to work through. And you're probably right that we shouldn't rush into marriage. But promise me something?"

"What?"

"You won't shut me out while you work through all of this. Let me help in any way I can, if I can."

Josie tipped her head back to look up at Scott. Gently touching his lips with her fingers, she just nodded her head. As a tear threatened to fall, she quickly laid her head back on his shoulder.

But he'd seen the tear. "Why are you crying, Josie? I don't want to make you cry."

"It's a girl thing," she replied.

"What?"

"We girls sometimes cry when we're happy," she explained softly.

"Oh." Scott wasn't going to say he understood that. Makes no sense at all, he thought. Why would you cry when you're happy?

Josie pulled back and smiled at him. "Think we should go in?"

"Okay. Do we want to tell them?"

"Tell them what?"

"That we're going to get married."

"I think we should give them time to get used to the fact that I'm a girl before we spring that on them. Let's just keep it between us for now. Okay?"

"Okay. But is it okay if they know I love you?" He leaned down to kiss her again. "I don't think I can keep that a secret from them."

Holding hands and smiling they walked through the kitchen into the living room. Cindy looked up at them and her mouth fell open, but nothing came out.

Scott laughed. "Wow. It's actually happened. Cindy is speechless."

At that both Jim and Barb turned to look at them. Barb smiled. "I hope you two don't think you're fooling anyone. It's written all over your faces."

"What is?" Scott feigned innocence.

"That won't fool your mother, Scott. You should know better than that." Jim was grinning.

"Okay. Okay. Just what is it that's written all over our faces, Mom?" Scott inquired. "Can't be that we're in love because we didn't know it until this afternoon."

Barb came over and hugged them both. "I thought I saw this coming. I'm very happy for both of you."

"Are you sure, Mrs. May.. er, Barb? My life is a total mess right now. You all may not want me in the family."

"Josie! We have learned to care for you a great deal these past few weeks. Your family mess, as you put it, isn't your fault, and you'll get it sorted out," Barb reassured her.

"When are you planning to get married?" Jim asked, his eyes twinkling. "We'll be happy to have you in the family, Josie. But I do think you two need some time."

"So, Josie insists," Scott complained. "She thinks we should wait at least two months."

Barb laughed. "Two months! That's hardly enough time to plan a wedding!"

"Actually, we haven't really talked about a date, yet," Josie replied. "I'm sure it will be more than two months, though."

"More?" Scott pretended to be crying. "More?"

Josie just laughed and took his hand. "If it's real, it'll keep. Isn't that the current wisdom on the subject?"

"Where did you hear that?" he demanded. "I've never heard that."

Grinning, Scott put his arm over her shoulder. "Boy, I'm being abused already."

After a few more minutes of foolishness, the conversation settled into real issues. Barb assured Josie that when the time came, they would be happy to help in any way with the wedding. "In fact, I've always felt a little cheated that I'd only get to plan one wedding, with only two daughters and one eloped. It would be fun to help you. Of course, dear, I know, your mom will want to be involved, too. I'm sure there'll be enough to do to keep both of us women busy."

"And, Josie, if things don't work out with your dad and you need someone to walk you down the aisle, I'd be proud to do the honors." Jim smiled at her as he shook hands with Scott. "Scott, I'm very happy for you."

LATER, AS SCOTT DROVE Josie back to the church to get her truck, they held hands and smiled. "This is nice," Scott admitted. "Very nice."

"Hmm."

"Josie, I cannot say I've ever known you to say so little. Are you sure you're okay?"

"I'm fine. I think I'm just afraid if I'm not very quiet I'll wake up and find it was only a dream."

"It's no dream, Josie. If it is, I don't want to wake up either."

"But it's all so sudden, so fast. What if we're wrong and it isn't real?"

"It's real," Scott assured her. "I know it's real."

He parked by her truck. They talked a few minutes then she got in her truck and shut the door. Scott opened her door, pulled her down for a quick kiss, then shut the door again. She smiled and started up the motor. As she pulled out of the parking lot, she could see Scott in her rear-view mirror, blowing kisses to her.

"I do love you, Scott," she said.

Chapter 17

PAMELA ANSWERED ON THE second ring. "Josie, I'm so glad to hear from you. How are you?"

They talked a bit, happy to be talking but a bit strained because of the newness of their relationship. This would take a while, obviously. Josie told her mother that she was trying to talk Hope into moving down to Rapid City, or Spearfish, to continue her schooling. Pamela said she and Hope had spoken on the phone for a few minutes earlier in the week. It only made her miss Hope more. She was hoping Hope could at least come down for a visit soon. They agreed it would be nice to get all three of them together, but they probably needed to take things one day at a time.

Josie had called Sam the night before, but he'd refused to speak to her. "I don't know what to do. I don't want things to stay this way between us. But we do have some things we need to talk out and he, obviously, doesn't want to talk about any of it."

She didn't tell her about Scott. It just seemed too soon.

Pamela had concerns about Hope's schooling. "I'm not sure which schools around here offer degrees in nursing," she said. "I could do some checking around if you'd like."

Josie agreed that they needed to know what Hope's options actually were. Also, was it too late to transfer with classes probably starting in September? Pamela wrote down all of their questions and promised to do the research.

After a few more minutes, Pamela brought up the subject Josie had been somewhat avoiding. "Josie, I'd really like for you to meet Patrick and our children. Would you like to come up and have dinner with us some evening?"

Josie felt she might be uncomfortable in Pamela's home right now, so they agreed to meet at a restaurant in Rapid City, since Josie didn't know her way around Spearfish. "Actually, I don't even know where Spearfish is, yet," she laughed. "I looked on a map after we talked the first time so I know it's north of Rapid City, but I wouldn't have the slightest idea of which road to take."

"We don't mind driving down and I really do want Patrick and the kids to meet you. Later, when you're more comfortable with us, it would be nice to have you come up. I don't know what your schedule is like, but you might be able to come to a soccer game now and again. We'll see. I'm not trying to rush things. I'm just so happy to have you back that I want to see you as much as I can." Pamela stopped for a breath. "Guess I'm talking too much again. My mom always did say I talk too much."

"It's okay, Mom. I should go and get things ready so I can get to work in the morning. But you guys will come down on Friday night, right?"

"Yes, dear. We'll meet you at the same Perkins. That way you don't have to try to find a different place."

As Josie got ready for bed, she felt like she was in a daze. So much had happened in the past few hours! Being with Scott just seemed so right, so perfect! His kisses are sweet. But they don't last long enough. I need more! She smiled at her own silliness. How sweet of his parents to accept me so readily and offer to help with the wedding. Wedding! I'm actually talking about getting married. I cannot believe all of this came about just today.

I knew last night at the Playhouse that Scott really was the man I thought I had gotten to know. But how sweet to know that it's mutual; he loves me, too. We really have to slow down and get better acquainted. We can't just jump into marriage. But he was so adorable when he asked me to marry him. I really wasn't expecting it; it's way too soon. But he feels it, too. We're just so right together.

She drifted to sleep somewhere in her sweet remembering. She woke up with a smile. Life is good. God is good. Wow. This is really something. If someone had told me a couple of months ago that all this would happen when I moved down here, I wouldn't have believed them.

If I'd known about Mom, I wonder what I'd have done. I think I'd have been afraid to confront the situation. Afraid of losing Dad's love. But I feel so much better about myself now that I know she didn't just walk away and never look back. She loved us. She tried to come back. She called. She wrote. I have my mother back.

She bounded out of bed, dressed quickly and ran down the steps to grab a bite for breakfast. Mrs. Stewart was in the dining room and asked if Josie needed a sack lunch today. Gratefully, Josie accepted the offer and took the lunch and breakfast back to her room. Opening her Bible to Mark, she read and nibbled on her breakfast. As she became more absorbed in the Bible, she forgot to eat. The alarm went off on her watch, reminding her it was time to leave for work. She quickly finished her breakfast and dropped to her knees by the chair. Remembering to pray was coming easy to her. Knowing how to pray was a little more difficult. Sometimes it was hard to say anything. Other times she felt like she just rambled on, hoping God was making some sort of sense out of it.

When she walked into the shop at work, Scott turned with a huge smile on his face and walked right over and put his arms around her and kissed her.

"Hmm."

"Good morning, Josie. I thought you'd never get here."

"I'm not late, am I?"

"No. Well, maybe. Where were you five years ago?" He grinned at the puzzled look on her face. "I think you're about five years late showing up in my life."

"Oh." She smiled. "Well, I'm really sorry about that, cowboy, but I got here as soon as I could."

"Cowboy?"

"I always wanted to say that." She laughed at herself. Leaning forward she reached up to collect another kiss and then pulled back. "Okay. We'd better get to work." She resolutely walked to the refrigerator and deposited her lunch.

"Okay. Boss man. What's first?"

"All business, now, huh? Okay. I'll be good." Scott picked up the stack of work orders. "This one needs to be first, Josie. Kind of an emergency."

Josie read the order, clarified a couple of points with Scott, loaded up and left. She'd taken a couple additional tickets so probably wouldn't be back before lunch. I'm sure it's better this way, she thought, grinning. I'll get a lot more work done, and so will Scott.

Scott watched her drive away with a huge grin spread all over his face. He could feel it. Isn't she wonderful? He asked himself. Then he answered. Yes. She is truly wonderful. She's sweet, she's strong, she's pretty, she loves Jesus, and she loves me.

Shaking himself, he reminded himself that he needed to get busy, he had several orders to fill; he needed to get the plans drawn so he could start building. But his mind was slow in making the transition. Finally, he got into the swing of things and made pretty good progress on the table he was designing for Mrs. Saltzman. He had all the pieces cut, all the hardware ready to go, and the stain picked out. The rest should be a breeze.

He was hard at work, drilling, sanding, attaching trim, and in general doing what he loved when Josie came back in for lunch. It took him only a couple of seconds to switch gears and welcome her with open arms, literally.

Josie smiled. "Does the boss know you behave this way with the hired help?"

"I think so," Scott said, grinning. "You know, I feel like an idiot. Every time I glance in a mirror or even just become aware of my face; I'm wearing an idiotic grin. I look like a simpleton."

"Oh, Scott. You have a beautiful smile. But I know what you mean. I can be doing anything and stop and think about it and, sure enough, I'm wearing a grin."

"Well, at least it isn't just me."

"Actually, I think it was probably very catching and you gave it to me when you kissed me."

"Oh, sure. Make it all my fault!" he pretended to grouse.

"Poor boy. Is everyone picking on you?" Josie kissed her fingertips and put them gently on Scott's lips. "If a kiss started it, maybe another kiss will keep it going?"

Scott leaned down and kissed her lightly. "Will that do it?"

"I think it will get me through the lunch hour anyway." Josie smiled and backed away to retrieve her lunch from the refrigerator.

"Do we have a lot for this afternoon, boss man?" she asked as she grabbed a soda from the machine and sat down.

"Actually, yes. The phone has rung at least a dozen times this morning and we have six or seven to try to do today. The others can wait for morning."

"Wow. You're really staying busy. Is it always this busy?"

"I usually stay steady but of course the summer is always busier. But I honestly think this is the busiest summer I've ever had. I think word is out that I have a very capable, and pretty, handyman."

"Yeah. Sure." Josie laughed.

"I'm only half joking," Scott insisted. "Some of the calls have actually asked me if they ordered the work would I be coming, or would I send you."

"Really?"

"Truly. This is a small community and word gets around. I think you're a genuine hit with the customers."

"And here I thought that being a girl was a big problem for me in this field," Josie said ruefully.

"The more I think about it, the more I see your point of view in initially getting hired. I'd really like to think I'd have hired you right off, regardless of your gender. But I'm not sure."

"So, even though the customers like me now, I may have been right to start out pretending to be a guy?"

"I'd hate to say that's right, it doesn't reflect too well on my gender. Also, I hate to say lying is the right thing to do. But, I'll admit, you may have at least been justified." Scott shook his head. "It doesn't say much for me that, even as a Christian who should be more open and caring, I might have been no better than anyone else in this situation."

"Well, we'll never know. I, for one, am so glad that whole thing is behind me and that I didn't lose your friendship or your folks' friendship, or my job over it. I don't know when I've been so happy to have something over and done with." Josie thought that might still be an understatement.

"I'm sure you are. And I don't want to beat it to death. But I do have a question for you. Please promise me you'll tell me the whole truth, okay?" Scott grinned.

Josie wasn't smiling. "So, you're always going to doubt what I say is the truth?"

"No." Scott took her hand. "Just on this one question. Humor me, okay?"

Josie pulled her hand away. "Sure. Go ahead."

"Is Josie your real name? Like, it's not short for something else?"

"No. It's Josie."

"Now the big question." Scott was still smiling. Josie still wasn't.

"Were you really named after Josie Wales?"

"That's your big question? You jerk!"

"Hey, Josie. I'm just being a goof ball. I didn't mean to make you mad." He took her hand again. "Well? Were you?"

"Yeah. I really was named after Josie Wales. Satisfied?"

"Josie? Are you really mad at me? I was just joking around."

Finally, Josie started to laugh, and Scott resumed breathing. "Wow. You had me scared. I was starting to think you were really mad at me."

"I was," Josie insisted. "I'm just not mad now."

"Okay. Can I push it just a little further?"

"What, now?"

"What's your middle name?"

"Crystal."

"That's pretty."

"So. . .?" Josie tipped her head a bit sideways. "Come on, give!"

"What?"

"What's your middle name?"

"Oh. It's James."

"For your dad?"

"Yeah. What's yours for?"

"If you'd asked me that a couple of months ago, I wouldn't have known the answer. Now I know it's my mom's maiden name."

"Cool."

"Okay. Enough of this. Let's get to work." Josie tossed her soda can into the recycle bag and threw her lunch sack away. "What's next, boss man?"

Josie left with several tickets and Scott returned to his work. The table he was building was coming along nicely but he was getting other orders that necessitated his finishing this project so he could get going on the others. Being busy was always good but being too busy was starting to be a bit stressful.

Of course, he thought, it would help if I could keep my mind on my work. I'm usually a much faster worker but I seem to be doing a lot of daydreaming these days. He smiled. Thinking about Josie is so much nicer than thinking about work. But it doesn't pay very well so I'd better get my attention on what I'm doing.

He hummed as he worked and was soon engrossed in his project. He cut, glued, nailed, and sanded throughout the afternoon.

Chapter 18

FRIDAY EVENING FOUND JOSIE parked at Perkins, watching for Pamela and her family. I'm really nervous, she thought. It's silly, I guess. No one is going to bite me. She smiled. At least I hope no one will. What is Patrick like? Wonder what he thought when Mom and I got together? Does he resent my presence in their lives, now? What about Eric and Andi? Wonder what they think about having a big sister.

"Josie?" Knocking on her window startled her out of her revere. Pamela and her family were waiting for her to get out of her truck so they could go in.

"Josie, this is my husband, Patrick."

Patrick offered his hand to Josie and when she reached to shake hands with him, he pulled her into a hug. "Hi, Josie. I've heard about you for years. I'm so glad we finally found you."

"This is Eric." Josie offered her hand and Eric shook it, very solemnly.

"You're my big sister, aren't you?" he asked.

"Yes, I am. I'm happy to meet you, Eric."

"And this is Andi."

Josie offered her hand but Andi kind of scooted behind Patrick.

"That's okay, Andi. I know it's kind of scary meeting a big sister you didn't even know you had."

They entered the restaurant and were seated in a large corner booth.

The first several minutes was taken up figuring out and placing their orders.

Everyone seemed a bit more settled down after the waitress left. The children, especially, had been watching Josie very closely and Josie was very aware of their scrutiny.

"So, Eric," she began. "Mom says you play soccer?"

His face lit up. "Yup. I'm the best player on my team!"

Patrick started to say something to him, but Pamela discreetly waved him off. Josie was paying direct attention to Eric and he seemed pleased.

"Are you, now? That's great. What position do you play?"

"We switch all the time. Our coach wants us to be able to play wherever we're needed," he said, importantly.

"Which position do you enjoy playing the most?"

"I think I'd like to grow up to be a goalkeeper," he responded. "It's the most important position."

Josie grinned. "Yeah. That's what I used to think, too."

"You played soccer?" Eric was obviously impressed. "Really? What position did you play?"

"Like you, we played all positions. I did play goalie sometimes but I played right forward most of the time."

Andi's reserve seemed to be slipping a bit. She joined the conversation. "I play soccer, too," she announced.

"You do? That's great! Do you play positions yet?" Josie asked.

"Yeah. No, I don't think so."

Patrick patted his daughter on her head. "We don't work on that very much, do we, sweetie?"

"Are you her coach, then?" Josie queried.

"Guilty as charged," he replied with a grin. "I love the sport and help the college coach so it's quite an adjustment to drop down to the little ones. But I think it's actually making me a better coach at both levels. And I love working with the kids."

The evening passed in pleasant, fairly neutral conversation. Pamela and her family left about 8:30 as the children were getting quite tired. It was about the right amount of time, Josie thought. Time enough to visit and get somewhat comfortable but not so long that you ran out of things to say. She suspected that another conversation, without the children, would get down to the nitty gritty more. But this was just right for a beginning.

They exchanged hugs with their good-byes; even Andi and Eric gave Josie bashful hugs as they left. Patrick, once again, enveloped her in a big, welcoming bear hug. "I'm so glad we found you, Josie. Welcome home."

Josie waved until they were back on Rushmore Road then climbed into her pickup to drive back to her rooming house.

I'm exhausted, she realized. What's so hard just eating dinner with some people? I feel like I climbed a mountain. But, she smiled, I also feel like I have a family. That was so nice. Patrick was certainly as nice as I could have hoped for. My stepfather. She giggled. Why does that word sound so sinister? I guess stepparents have taken a bum rap, but lots of them must be like Patrick.

When she got up to her room and got her shoes off, she settled back on her bed and called Hope. They only talked a few minutes, but Josie wanted to let Hope know about Patrick and the kids.

"They're sweet, Hope. Kind of shy but I would be, too, in their place. Patrick couldn't have been nicer."

Hope had some questions about Pamela, and they spoke a little more on that. Then Josie had a question for Hope.

"Have you given any more thought to moving down here?"

Hope was thinking about it, had talked to Pamela about it, but was kind of waiting to see what she could get into for the fall session. "Mom said she'd try to find out everything she could by Monday."

"Josie? I called Dad last week and he hung up on me."

"Me, too," Josie agreed.

"I'm going to drive home tomorrow morning and see if he'll see me in person."

"Good luck."

"Do you think it's the right thing to do?"

"Hope, I have no idea. I don't know if he's just going to stay mad no matter what we do of if he's just waiting for us to come home and sit him down and force him to listen to us tell him we still love him."

"I do still love him, Josie, but I'm not sure I like him very well right now."

"I agree. And he's sure not making it any easier for us."

"Well, I'll let you know how it goes," Hope said as they hung up.

"Hello," Josie sort of whispered into the phone.

"Josie? You okay?"

"Who wants to know?"

"Okay. You're awake enough to be sassy so you're awake enough to get up," Scott said, laughing.

"Why do I have to get up? I don't have to work today."

"I know. But it's such a beautiful day that I thought maybe we could drive up through the Northern Black Hills."

"Is there anything to do besides ride around?"

"What else would you like to do?" he teased.

"You're the guide, you tell me," she responded.

"Okay. We can stop whenever we like and get out and walk. We can drive down through Spearfish Canyon and go to Roughlock falls. Then we can climb down and go to Spearfish Waterfall. In Deadwood there's a pretty famous cemetery where you can see the head stones for Calamity Jane and Wild Bill Hickock. We could. . .."

"Did you say Spearfish?"

"Yes. Do you want to explore Spearfish since you've never been there, and your mom lives there?"

"Could we?"

"Sure. The other day when I delivered that chest of drawers I stopped at AAA and picked up a map for Spearfish."

"Scott! That's great! What time do you want to go?"

"Do you have a lot of stuff to do today or can you take most of the day to explore?"

"I need to do some laundry but that's all. I can do it later, I think. Let's just goof off today, okay?"

"Sounds good. What if I pick you up about 10?"

"I'll be ready."

"Be sure to bring shoes you can get wet in case we want to walk around the falls, Ok?"

"Okay. See you soon." This is more like it, she thought, getting ready for a date with my boyfriend. And the smile was back.

AS THEY DROVE UP I-90 toward Spearfish, Josie tried to find her mother's address on the map. Every time she'd get close to the coordinates for the street, Scott would point out something to her and she'd lose her place. When they pulled into Spearfish, Scott pulled over so they could figure out where they wanted to go. They'd decided to drive around a bit, just to let Josie get a little bit familiar with the town, but to also try to find Pamela's home. They didn't plan to stop, just find it so Josie actually knew where her mother was.

They stopped at the Dairy Queen for ice cream cones and continued driving, finding the college and the major stores. Finally, they got serious about finding Pamela's place. They found the street and were going slow so Josie could check the numbers on the houses when they heard someone yelling. Josie looked past Scott and saw Patrick waving to them. Scott pulled over and Patrick came to the car.

"Hey, I'm glad you all came up. Come on in."

"Oh, no," Josie stammered. "We weren't going to stop. We're just driving around and decided to find where you guys live."

"Well, that's okay. I know Pam will want to see you and so will the kids. Come on in," Patrick insisted.

So, Scott parked and they went inside with Patrick. Pamela's smile was instant and genuine. "Josie! I'm so glad to see you!" She hugged her daughter then turned to Scott. "Hello."

Josie introduced Scott and then the kids came in, so she introduced him to Eric and Andi.

"Is he your boyfriend?" Andi asked.

"Andi! It's not polite to ask such questions," Pamela scolded.

Scott only laughed. "I'll answer that question, gladly, young Andi. I am, indeed, her boyfriend."

"Ooh!" Andi was grinning from ear to ear. "He's handsome, Josie."

"Yes, he is," Josie agreed, smiling at him. "Do you think I should keep him, Andi?"

Andi only nodded her head, but she was still smiling.

Pamela offered them iced tea and cookies, until she realized how late it was, then she changed the offer to lunch. Josie wasn't comfortable dropping in uninvited and then staying to lunch, so she declined for them. But Pamela and Patrick both insisted they stay. They had promised the kids to cook hot dogs and hamburgers outside and they had plenty. After lunch Josie and Scott took their leave, explaining that they wanted to do some more exploring.

"I want to show her Roughlock Falls," Scott said. "It's always been one of my favorite spots and I haven't been there yet this summer."

"The Canyon is beautiful, too," Pamela agreed. "You'll have to be sure she sees it again with the fall leaves."

Josie told Pamela that Hope was supposed to be going home this weekend. "Dad won't talk to either of us on the phone so she's going to see if she gets any further in person. I'll let you know how it goes after she calls me."

"I LIKE HER," SCOTT said as they drove away. "I really like Patrick, too."

"Yes, he's been so nice to me. I wondered if he'd resent me but when I first met him, he said they'd been trying to find me, then he said, 'welcome home'. He seems to care about me and that's so neat."

"Are you worried about Hope this weekend?" Scott asked. "Do you think your dad would get violent?"

"I would never have thought so before but he's acting so strange that I just don't know what to expect. I am a little concerned for Hope. Mostly, that if Dad won't see her, she'll be so upset. I'm anxious to hear from her."

Scott suggested they pull over and pray for Hope and Josie gratefully agreed. They asked God for protection for Hope and also for wisdom that she not try to resolve everything all at once by herself.

Later, after they'd climbed down to the Falls and splashed each other and then raced back to the top, they started back for Rapid City. Pleasantly tired, they were content with their company and spoke very little, both somewhat lost in their thoughts.

Sunday evening Hope called Josie. "Josie, he's crazy! He wouldn't let me in at first. Then when he did let me in, he refused to let me go beyond the kitchen, not even to use the bathroom. He said that if we want our things out of that house that we have to come and get stuff next weekend. After that, anything he finds of ours he will throw away. Also, after that, neither of us will be welcome there again." Hope was crying.

Josie was crying, too. "Oh, Hope. Won't he ever listen to us? How could he have been so good to us for all those years and now kick us out?"

"I don't know. You're right. In many ways he was a very good father to us, and I love him. I'm still upset about what he did to us where Mom's concerned, but we could work past that if he'd only let us."

"I love him, too. I'm upset with him, but, like you say, we should be able to work our way through all of this. I don't know what to do now."

"Well, we're going to have to figure out how to get there next weekend and get all of our stuff."

"This would be a good time to move you down here, Hope. What do you think?"

"Yeah, if I had someplace to move into. I think I can get into school there from what Mom said the other day. She's getting me the applications I need. Do you think you could find me somewhere to live by next Friday?"

They agreed that Josie would talk to Pamela and see about housing in Spearfish and Josie would check the papers in Rapid City. They would have to decide what they were going to do very shortly. Hope could get most of her belongings in her little car and Josie would be there with her truck and might have room for some of Hope's stuff.

Josie called Pamela and explained the situation. Pamela said they had an extra room downstairs and that Hope could stay there while she looked for what she wanted. They wondered if there was any dorm space available and Pamela said she'd call to find out.

Scott had tried to call while Josie was talking to Pamela, so Josie called him back. She explained the whole situation to him.

"Josie, what if I drove my truck up, along with you in your truck? We could get your stuff and Hope's in the two trucks and then caravan with Hope back down here."

"Well, that might work," Josie hesitated. "That's an awful imposition, though."

"Not when I offered. We could leave real early Saturday morning, get loaded and then get a couple of motel rooms, one for me and one for you girls. Then, we could come back down on Sunday."

Josie called Hope back and they agreed to the plan. Hope was hesitant about staying with Pamela since she still hadn't seen her and hadn't met Patrick and the kids; but agreed that, short term, it might be her best option.

"Okay, then it's settled. Will that give you enough time there, Josie? If you think we should, we could drive up Friday night?" Scott asked.

"I'm not sure. Can we decide in a day or so? I kind of need to see how it will work for Hope."

"No problem. I'll see you in the morning at work. Sleep well."

Scott said goodnight and said he was blowing her a kiss.

Silly man, Josie thought and smiled. Sweet man.

Chapter 19

Scott closed shop at noon on Friday and he and Josie, in their separate vehicles, left for Billings. They stopped a few times along the way to visit, explore, grab a soda or just walk around a bit. They could do nothing else that day besides arrive in Billings so it didn't matter if they got there early or late, other than how tired they might be.

Hope was driving over from Missoula but wouldn't get there until later as it was further, and she couldn't leave until about three. Josie had called ahead to get motel rooms for them, and they would meet Hope there.

Scott had never been in Montana so was interested in the scenery along the way but was surprised at how far apart the towns were.

"Montana is a large state," Josie said. "Especially to drive from one side to the other."

"So, I see," Scott replied. "I didn't pay that much attention in school, I guess."

They arrived in Billings around eight, checked into their rooms, and took Josie's truck to find a place to eat supper. Then Josie drove around the city, showing Scott where she'd gone to elementary and high school as well as the trade school she'd attended. They drove past Sam's house but there were no lights. "I sure hope he's there in the morning so we can get our stuff," Josie worried. "It would be nice if we could visit a little, but Hope's report didn't sound too favorable."

"Let's pray that he'll be receptive, at least to you girls getting your stuff out," Scott suggested. They held hands and asked the Lord for His help and guidance for the next couple of days.

Hope arrived just before midnight. They didn't stay up and visit much; Josie introduced Scott and Hope and then everyone turned in for the night, agreeing to go for breakfast by eight.

Saturday after they'd eaten, they all drove to Sam's and, cautiously, knocked on the door. After a long wait, Sam let them in. Josie introduced Scott and Sam reluctantly shook his hand but refused any small talk. He told the girls to get their stuff loaded up and he went out the back door, slamming the screen shut.

"This isn't good," Josie whispered. "I was so hoping he'd be willing to talk to us."

"We prayed, Josie. God's in charge. This isn't over yet. Let's get your belongings loaded and then we'll try again," Scott encouraged the girls. Josie nodded but Hope looked at her and Scott with bewilderment.

As the girls went through their rooms and took the things they knew were theirs, they left all furniture behind. They would like to have taken their beds and desks but, without Sam's permission, they were reluctant to do so. Still, they each had cedar chests, closets full of clothes, pictures, books, shoes and jewelry they'd left behind. As they were finishing up with those items, Sam came in and looked in their rooms.

"Better take those beds, desks and dressers," he ordered. "I'll just haul them to the dump if you leave them here. I don't want anything in this house to remind me of either of you."

Josie sat down in the middle of the room and started crying. Glaring at Sam, Scott went to her and put his arm around her shoulder. "Josie, don't cry. It won't solve anything. Let's just get this stuff loaded and get on the road towards home."

They had to unload the pickups to put the furniture in and then repack the rest of the stuff around it. When they were finally loaded up, Scott said, "Okay, ladies. Shall we see if Sam will talk now? Maybe he'd let us treat him to lunch."

They went back through the house and found Sam on the back porch. He refused to go to lunch with them, telling them to hit the road. Josie went to him, knelt at his knees and begged, "Please, Dad. Don't make this be the way we say goodbye."

"Not my choice. You girls have chosen this path."

"No, Dad. We don't want to lose you. We love you. You're all we had growing up and you were a great Dad to us," Hope said, crying. "Please, Dad. Can't we talk about all of this?"

Sam finally relented and the girls asked some questions about when Pamela had left. Sam gave short, curt, replies at first. He did gradually relax a bit and the conversation opened up more. Scott started to go outside but both the girls motioned for him to stay.

When the girls brought up the topic of the cards and letters their mother had sent that Sam had refused, he got very defensive and angry. Josie kept going, steadily bringing up the facts that she, herself, knew to be true. Holding her breath, she said, "She sent stuff to us for five years and finally stopped. But she saved them all and gave them back to us. I also have copies of her phone bills that show the calls she made to us that we never received."

Sam blustered, "What are you talking about? She didn't call here except when you talked to her."

"Her phone bills show calls to us monthly for the first five years she was gone."

Sam crumpled. "OK. OK. So, I'm the worse dad in the world. What did you expect me to do? She left us for another man."

"No, Dad. She didn't. Her mother was sick, and she died. That Dylan that you were worried about only went back to Spearfish because he was very ill. He died a couple of months after our grandmother did. Mom only saw him once and that was at the hospital when Grandma died. She told you all about that."

Josie was past anger and could only feel sadness. How much they'd all missed because of a misunderstanding. She'd always missed her mother but now she felt like she'd lost her father, too.

Sam began to weep. "I'm so sorry. I really thought I was doing what was best for all of us." Josie walked over to him and put her arms around him. She held him but she couldn't seem to say what he needed to hear. It wasn't all right. They'd all suffered, but he'd been the one who had kept everyone apart. The one who had lied to Hope and her, repeatedly, through the years. I know I'm supposed to forgive him, she thought. But I don't know if I can. But if I don't, I'll lose him, too. Oh, dear God, please help me.

Josie looked over at her sister. Hope sat with a glazed look on her face, staring off into nothingness.

"Hope?" Josie called to her softly. When Hope looked up, Josie reached out her arm to her. Slowly, Hope stood and came over and Josie put her arm around her. Hope began to sob so Josie just held on tight. So much pain. So much heartache.

With the bulk of the truth finally out and the worst of the tears cried, she hoped, Josie got everyone to sit down again and they discussed the situation at length. Sam reluctantly answered his daughters' questions, occasionally wiping a tear from his eyes. The more he told them the more questions they had. Josie interjected some of the answers she knew from their mother.

Sam didn't refute anything Pamela had said and seemed surprised at some of what Josie related to them.

The conversation finally seemed to be over. Everyone was drained and no one seemed to know where to go from there.

"I'm hungry," Sam finally stated. "Anyone else?"

The girls and Scott agreed, and they ordered some pizza. Everyone kind of scattered, using the bathroom, washing faces, etc. until the pizza arrived. Then they sat down at the table and talked more while they ate. Sam seemed to have regained his poise somewhat and tried joking with the girls. Their halfhearted laughter sounded hollow in the home that felt empty.

One thing Josie had gotten straight was the existence of Aunt Helen. Sam admitted that she was a friend he'd known since he was a child. There was nothing between them, but he thought it seemed more honorable for the girls to think she was their aunt. She'd agreed to be there for the girls because she had raised daughters and loved kids.

As they prepared to leave, Josie told Sam that she and Scott planned to marry but not right away and asked if he would come to her wedding and give her away. He flatly refused.

"You're an idiot to get married," he said to her. "All you'll get out of it is heartache."

"I believe God will help us build a strong marriage," Josie said softly. "If we're honest with each other and worship God together, we will be fine."

"God!" Sam shouted. "What's He got to do with anything?"

"He loves me; He died for me, and He's forgiven me and given me eternal life," Josie said firmly. "He's awesome!"

"God." Sam said derisively. "You're a fool."

Sam was not to be convinced and the girls and Scott said their good-byes and started down the road to Rapid City.

It hadn't been pretty, but it was, for now anyway, over. This chapter of their lives was now a part of their past.

Chapter 20

JOSIE WAS SITTING ON the front porch with her cell phone at her ear when Scott pulled up. As he approached her, he heard her tell Hope, good-bye.

"So, how's Hope doing?" he asked. "She is getting along okay with your mom and her family?"

"Actually, she's going to be moving in with some other girls from college," Josie reported. "In the six weeks since she got there, Mom and Patrick have had a constant flow of college students from their church at the house. They wanted to help her get acquainted here. Today, Hope agreed to share apartment expenses with three of the gals she's become friends with. She's excited, I think."

"That's good, isn't it? That she'll have someplace away from your family."

"I think Hope enjoyed staying with Mom and the family, but it was a bit awkward since they didn't really know each other. But it's helped them get acquainted and she's loved getting to know Eric and Andi."

"How much Christian influence have the church college kids had on Hope, do you know?" Scott smiled. "It can't have hurt, I wouldn't think."

"Hope hasn't said a lot about it, but I think she's giving it a lot of thought. We grew up with no church and certainly no Bible knowledge. It's a big change, a good one, but still it's major. It's completely changed how I think about things," Josie explained.

"Yes, it affects your entire world view," Scott agreed. "I didn't realize the value of that until after I was out of school. I think when you're still in school you're trying so hard to become separate people from your parents that you sort of discard much of what they've taught you. I had to re-evaluate what

I'd learned at home and at church, compare it to what the Bible said, and determine if that was what I believed. You cannot live on someone else's faith. I had to find my own."

Josie and Scott joined hands and started walking around the neighborhood. It had become a pleasant way to spend time together, to talk over ideas and suggestions, and to get better acquainted. It was the middle of October, so the leaves were changing and falling, and Josie thought the world looked absolutely beautiful. She acknowledged that being in love might have something to do with it.

"Want to drive down through Spearfish Canyon tomorrow and check out Roughlock Falls again, now with the fall colors?" Scott asked.

Josie nodded her head, dreamily. "That would be lovely."

They walked and talked some more then kissed goodnight and Scott left her on the porch and he drove home. His heart was still on the porch with Josie and his mind was certainly on the love of his life.

I never knew it could be like this, he mused. I cannot imagine living my life without her. Wonder how soon we could get married? I wonder if PJ has classes that we must attend. I'd better ask, I guess.

SATURDAY WAS A BEAUTIFUL day and Scott and Josie enjoyed their drive through the canyon. When they got to the falls, they put on their climbing shoes and climbed to the bottom and then walked across the water on the big rocks.

"This is so beautiful," Josie called to Scott. "I can't believe you can actually get right behind the water."

"Wanna work your way around behind the falls?" Scott asked, grinning. "Bet you're chicken."

Josie was tempted to rise to the bait but just wasn't sure how wet she wanted to get since they still planned to eat somewhere. "Let me wait for a warmer day," she begged. "I don't want to get wet today."

Their day was relaxing and enjoyable and yet provided opportunities to discuss many subjects that either were important or would be important to them and their future life together. As they drove back into Rapid City, they were pleasantly tired but not quite ready to part company.

"Josie, how about I swing past my house. I know you've never seen the inside and, hopefully, that's where we'll live," Scott said, then quickly added, "But if you don't want to live there, we can sell it and get something else."

"Okay, let's go take a look," she agreed.

As Scott pulled into his driveway, he was mentally reviewing his house to know if the place was tidy or if he'd run through on his way out the other door, leaving items along the way.

"We'll go in through the front door although I've gotten into the habit of using the back door since it's close to where I park my truck," he explained as he unlocked the door. "It's not real big, only two bedrooms, but it was all I needed."

As they toured, Scott explained why one thing was a certain way, another different, identified pictures of relatives and friends, and generally enjoyed himself. Master of the manor, so to speak.

Josie looked at the house from a more feminine point of view, of course, and checked out the laundry room, the kitchen range and the bathrooms with great interest.

Finally, Scott could stand it no more. "Well? What do you think?"

"It's a very nice house, Scott. Did you do a lot of the work or did you buy it as is?"

Scott explained which things he'd altered or built in and which things were there when he bought the home. Then they went out the back door and into the garage, which didn't have room for a car as it was full of Josie's furniture and other belongings they'd moved back from Montana. They had only unloaded into the garage as they'd been too tired to do anything more. "Someday, hopefully, the gal I let store her stuff here will move in and I can have my garage back," he joked with Josie.

"Aha. So that's it! You only want to marry me so you can get your garage emptied out," Josie said with a grin. "Should have known."

"Is that a garden plot over there in the corner, Scott?" Josie asked as she started walking in that direction.

"I tried a garden the first couple of years but I always forgot to water it and I hated pulling weeds, so I gave up," Scott admitted sheepishly. "Do you think you might want to plant a garden?"

"Maybe. We used to have one and I enjoyed the fresh vegetables in the summer. But I'd also like some flowers."

"Over here on the side is where I'd imagined flowers growing but I never figured out what I wanted to plant there so it's still bare."

They spent an hour or so discussing different things they might want to do differently, or the same, inside the house and out.

"So, you think you'd like to live here, Josie?"

"Yes. At least for a while, it should serve us well. I like the big shade trees, too. Do they keep the place cool in the summer?"

"They help. But I did install central air last summer when I got tired of not sleeping on those hot July and August nights. I really enjoy it."

"Good thing I didn't know that last summer. I'd have been over here in your spare room," Josie joked.

"Do you think it's too early to think about a wedding date?" Scott asked hopefully. "We also need to check with PJ as he may want us to go to classes or counseling with him."

"Okay. Let's see what he says first then we can decide about a date," Josie agreed. "I don't think we want to look at anything before February because, as your mom said, it will take time and I sure don't want to try to do a wedding along with Christmas."

"I'm sure you're right. I'd love for it to be sooner, but we do have a lot to take care of before we actually get married. Let's see if we can talk to PJ after service in the morning, okay?"

Josie agreed.

"Josie, I want to get you a ring, but I don't know if you'd like to pick it out yourself or if you want me to do it on my own. We should have done that this afternoon instead of looking at the house."

"No, I'm glad we looked at the house. I enjoyed it and now I can visualize our home and make plans with a real house in mind. I would love to come with you to pick a ring. But I don't want something big and expensive; something dainty would be lovely."

"Okay. I'm sure there are jewelry stores in the mall, and they would be open evenings. I'm not sure how late the downtown stores stay open. Want to go look Monday night?"

When they had agreed to a Monday evening shopping trip, Scott took Josie home.

As he kissed her good-bye he said, "Hmm. This is nice. But I'll be glad when I don't have to kiss you good-bye. When we're Mr. & Mrs. Scott Mayforth. How does that sound to you?"

"Why are you so sure I want to take your name?" Josie asked him, looking pretty solemn.

"Oh! I hadn't thought of it. Do you plan to keep your name?" Scott wasn't too happy with that thought; it had never occurred to him that Josie wouldn't take his name.

"No. I will be proud to take your name. But you'd never asked me, so I had to give you a little bit of a hard time." She grinned.

"You're getting even with me for that middle name thing, aren't you?"

"No. I just didn't want you to leave yet," she admitted. "But I do have laundry to do and I want to reread the scripture for our Sunday School class. So, I guess I'd better go in and get started."

Scott kissed her again, held her for a minute or two more and then left. Josie waved until he turned the corner then went upstairs to get busy.

Chapter 21

WITH A DATE SET for February 5th, Josie called her dad to see if he would come to the wedding and give her away. As he had before, he flatly refused to be a part of it. They were getting along a little better in the past few weeks, but it was still a strained relationship. After a few awkward moments, Josie told him she loved him and hung up.

Hope would be her maid of honor, Scott's sister, Cindy would be a bridesmaid, and Andi would be a Jr. Bridesmaid. Scott would have Terry as his best man, Tim Adamson and Eric as his groomsmen. A couple of Scott's teammates would serve as ushers. Patrick would give Josie away since Sam refused. Pamela was shopping for the perfect 'mother of the bride' dress and had helped Josie find dresses for the bridesmaids.

Scott's mom, Barb, was helping Josie pick out flowers and a wedding cake and both Pam and Barb were helping with the wedding guest list and the invitations. The two women had become quite friendly during the past several weeks and enjoyed helping with the wedding. It was the first time, for each of them, to plan a wedding and they approached it with both wonder and amazement. "How in the world did they get this old so fast?"

CHRISTMAS WAS FAST APPROACHING, and the two families had agreed to share the holiday. They would go to the church in Rapid City for the Christmas Eve service and then all have Christmas dinner at Pam and Patrick's in Spearfish. Since Pam and Patrick had young children, they all felt it would be best for them to be in their own home. Brenda, Lance and Robbie would be with Lance's family this year, but Terry and Cindy would join the families in Spearfish, somewhat reluctantly.

"Mom, we don't even know them," Cindy had objected, and Terry had questioned it also. But both agreed that, for Scott and Josie, they could all be together this year, with the idea that Josie and her family would join them the next Christmas.

Pamela and Patrick were both in choir in their church, so everyone was planning to go to the Spearfish church the Sunday before Christmas for their choir production.

It was all quite overwhelming for both Josie and Hope. Sam had never made much out of birthdays or Christmas, so this was a totally new experience for them. For Josie, it was even more special because she now knew the real meaning of Christmas and felt she'd received the greatest gift ever given, in having Jesus as her Savior. Having Scott and his family and her own family around her made her feel as though she'd finally come home, even though it was a rather noisy 'home'.

TWO DAYS BEFORE CHRISTMAS Josie received a small package from Sam with gifts for her and Hope. They'd sent him a package a week or so before but didn't expect to hear from him. Josie put the gifts in the sack she was using to take her gifts to Pamela's and forgot about them.

WHEN THEY DROVE UP to Spearfish for the Choir production, Josie took along the gifts she had ready so Pam could put them under their tree. "I have more to wrap but I'll just have to bring them up Christmas morning, okay?" she said to Pamela. "I've never had this many people to buy gifts for," she said giggling. "This is so great! Having a nice big family to love."

Pamela held her daughter tenderly. "You don't know how happy I am to have my two big girls with me this Christmas." She wiped a tear from her eye. "I think Hope is starting to like me, now. For a long time, I don't think she trusted me."

"I think we were both a little afraid to trust you after all Dad had said for so many years. But we love having you back in our lives. We just wish we could get something settled with Dad. Even though he was wrong to lie to us like he did, he was still a very good father to us, and we love him. Right now, I don't know that I like him very well. But I do love him."

"Of course, you do, sweetie. You should. Sam will come around. He can only lose both of you if he doesn't. He's not that kind of a fool," she reassured her daughter. Silently she hoped she wasn't just fooling them both.

THE MUSIC AND DRAMA were outstanding and as Josie sneaked a glance at Hope, she saw tears in her eyes. Maybe finally Hope is starting to understand, she thought. Oh, dear Father, help her see how much she needs you.

There were cookies and either hot cider or punch downstairs after the performance. It was pretty crowded so most of Josie and Scott's families grabbed a cookie and headed outside. It was brisk with a light snow falling but no wind. "It's beautiful!" Hope sighed. "It looks just like a picture on a Christmas card."

"Currier and Ives," Barb said softly.

"Huh?" Many faces looked at her in bewilderment, but Pamela just smiled and agreed.

"Yes, it's lovely."

Christmas morning after everyone had eaten freshly made cinnamon rolls and scrambled eggs and drank coffee, juice or both, Eric and Andi were impatient. "Can we open our presents, now?" they begged.

Barb looked at Pamela with a question in her eyes. Pamela nodded and, standing up from the table, she reached for her Bible. "Now, kids, you know we always read the Bible story first."

Everyone scrambled for a place on the couch, in a chair or on the floor. Patrick took the Bible and opened to Luke 2. Josie had read the passage several times during the past few weeks but loved hearing Patrick read it again. She glanced at Hope to see her reaction and saw that she was totally engrossed in the Biblical account of the first Christmas. After Patrick set the Bible aside, they talked briefly about the awesome gift of Christmas.

Then Patrick started picking packages up from under and around the tree and having either Eric or Andi hand them out. After everyone had a gift, they all opened them, showed them off and gave appropriate thanks. Scott got up to help so the kids could sit a while and a few more rounds of gift opening were shared. Cindy and Terry were pleased that they, too, had gifts under the tree. Their family gifts had been brought up and Pamela and Patrick had also gifted them. Suddenly, Josie became aware of Hope's, "ooh, wow!"

"What is it, Hope?" she asked. Everyone stopped what they were doing and looked in Hope's direction. She held up a string of pearls.

"Those are beautiful!" Josie said. "Who are they from?"

"Dad. There's a note here; oh, he says that these were his mother's and that he's sent you something as well. He leaves it to us, we can trade gifts, or keep them how he sent them."

"Wow. That's great. I didn't even know he had anything like that from his mother. Wonder what he sent me!" Josie said, softly. "I sure wasn't expecting anything like this."

Patrick looked through the remaining gifts and found the one for Josie from Sam. "Here you go, Josie. Let's see what he sent you."

It was a wedding ring set. "Oh, Hope. Look!"

"You know, your grandmother, Peggy, was a great lady," Pamela said. "I really loved her. She treated me like the daughter she never had, and I missed her terribly after she died."

"When was that, Mom?" Hope asked.

"You girls were still very small. She was only in her seventies, but she'd gotten diabetes when she was about fifty and just couldn't seem to get a handle on it. She had complications, liver damage, etc. and just wasted away. It was a great sorrow to both Sam and myself. Her husband, Lou, had been hit by a car and killed instantly a few years before Peggy died."

"That must have been very hard for Sam," Patrick said. "You did say he was an only child, didn't you?"

"Yes. He actually had a sister who was stillborn but of course he grew up as an only," Pamela said. "I think he was very lonely as a child and after Peggy died, it was worse for him."

"Poor Dad," Josie said. "Now he's alone again."

"Yes. But, remember, this time it was his choice," Scott said. "You girls tried. I know. I was there."

"Yes. We're still praying, though," said Josie. "We haven't given up on him."

The conversation turned back to the lovely gifts Sam had sent the girls. Since Scott and Josie had already chosen and purchased her engagement and wedding rings, Hope opted to take the ring set. Josie felt the pearls would be perfect with her wedding gown and both mothers agreed.

When the gifts were all opened and admired and the paper cleared away, the two mothers headed for the kitchen to check on dinner. When Hope and Josie offered to help, they were told they weren't needed yet. So, the girls stayed in the living room and watched, with pleasure, their sister and brother enjoying their gifts. Not sure what to get them for Christmas the girls had gone together and bought a set of books about sport heroes who had faced difficulties in their search for success. They were written for youngsters and had lots of pictures along with some funny stories about them as well. Eric and Andi were both looking through the books and exclaiming over names they recognized.

Cindy, too, had risen to help in the kitchen but was also told she was to just relax and enjoy herself. So she also watched the kids with their gifts. She realized that soon her little nephew, Robbie, would be old enough for cool books and soccer balls.

Scott had gotten them each a new soccer ball and they were happy with the gifts but had to wait for the snow to melt. They were both willing to play in snow but the new snow, on top of what they already had, had given them snow about twenty inches deep; even the most ardent soccer fan has to admit defeat in the face of that depth.

DINNER WAS A PLEASANT, but noisy, affair that both Hope and Josie enjoyed. It was a very different experience for both of them, having grown up with only themselves and Sam for company. The sheer volume of conversation, itself, was somewhat intimidating so they were both quiet, just listening as their new family and Scott's family chatted as though they'd known each other for years. Even Terry and Cindy joined in, to Scott's delight, and expressed their opinions on the various topics that came up.

Josie sought Hope's eye and they grinned at each other, shrugged their shoulders, and resumed eating a most delicious repast. Barb had baked rolls that were being enjoyed now and pies that would be saved for a little later. Pamela and Patrick had cooked the rest of the meal.

"You're awfully quiet, Josie," Barb said. "You doing okay?"

"Oh, yes," Josie said. "This is delicious. But I've never seen so much food at one time before."

"Barb laughed. "Well, I think you'll have to get used to it, Josie, dear. My family has always loved the full complement of foods for the holidays."

"Mine, too," Pamela added. "Josie, we had fairly big dinners for Christmas when you and Hope were little. I'm sure you just don't remember."

"Nope. I sure don't," Josie agreed. "Do you, Hope?"

"I don't think so," Hope replied. "But you know how we've talked about Christmas and birthdays when we were kids. I just don't seem to remember any special days while Mom was still with us. Sorry, Mom."

"That's okay. I'm sure the trauma of thinking your mother just left you and didn't care for you any more was enough for you to deal with. I think God protects us from overload by letting us forget things that we either don't have any more or were difficult for us."

"I think He does, too," Barb agreed. "He knows how much we can handle, even with His help."

AFTER DINNER WAS OVER and the dishes either washed or put into the dishwasher, Patrick suggested they play a game. They finally decided the only game they had that would accommodate that many people was Monopoly. Eric and Andi didn't want to play and were excused to watch a video they'd received from Pamela and Patrick.

The rest of the group gathered around the dining room table and picked Patrick as their banker. The game got pretty noisy as Scott and Jim both started buying hotels and charging huge rents on their properties. Terry joined right in putting hotels on his properties but Cindy was more cautious, buying only one house.

Neither Josie nor Hope had ever played so it took them a while to get into the game and by then they were both nearly broke. With the more experienced players getting more and more aggressive the girls opted to just watch for a while. But by the time the game actually ended it was far too late to start another.

Reluctantly, everyone started gathering up their things and getting ready to depart. They'd had pie part way through the Monopoly game, and everyone was still complaining that they were too full.

"Sounds like a personal problem to me," Patrick said, laughing. "I mean, it's not like the ladies held a gun to anyone's head to force them to eat."

With many cries of, "Thank you and Merry Christmas," they all gradually dispersed. Hope had the shortest ride home as she was living in Spearfish. The Mayforths and Josie had the fifty-mile drive to Rapid City.

"THIS WAS THE NICEST Christmas ever," Josie said as Scott helped her carry her gifts in and up to her room. "I kind of hate that it's over already."

"It isn't," Scott assured her. "Christmas isn't over until January 6th."

"It isn't?" Josie was puzzled.

"You know, the 12 days of Christmas."

"Oh. Okay. I can handle that. It always seemed that you looked forward to it for weeks and then, suddenly, it was over. It always made me sad."

"Don't be sad, Josie, Christmas lives on in our hearts always because Jesus is ever with us."

Scott held Josie close. "Josie, this is the best Christmas ever. I do love you. I'll be so glad when I don't have to say goodnight and leave you. I'm going to love waking up to your pretty face."

"Can I still work for you?" Josie said, smiling up at Scott. "Or do you think that would be too much togetherness?"

They'd talked about it before, that Josie wanted to keep working at least for a while, and Scott thought they were a good team. But they both wanted a family, although not right away, and agreed that when they had children, it would be essential for Josie to be home with them.

So, Josie was just teasing Scott and he loved it.

"I think I could stand to work with you for a while longer," he teased. "At least, unless you start trying to run the shop."

"And what would be wrong with that? Don't you think I could run the shop?"

Scott kissed her. "Shh, Josie." Then he kissed her again.

"Hmm," Josie murmured. "Again."

Scott held her close. "Oh, Josie. I do love you."

"Me too," she said, laying her head on his shoulder. "But I think you better go home."

"I know. What do you want to do tomorrow, since we aren't working?"

They decided to spend some time at Scott's house getting some things moved to make room for Josie's belongings. They'd decided to use the bed Josie had brought from Montana in their guestroom but to use the dresser for themselves. Josie's cedar chest would also go in their room, but the desk would be placed in the guestroom for now.

Their wedding invitations were being mailed the next Monday and they had registered at a couple of local stores. Knowing that they would probably receive some gifts before the wedding they were deciding where to put those items so their families and friends could see and admire them.

Terry's birthday was the 26th so they were having dinner with Scott's family that night but decided to work at the house most of the day.

Chapter 22

JOSIE THOUGHT THE REHEARSAL had gone well. She'd never been to one before, so she had nothing to base her conclusion on. The organist at the church had been most helpful in selecting the music and finding a singer. Barb and Pamela had helped Josie determine the help she would need at the reception, like someone to serve the cake, pour coffee, serve punch, etc.

Barb and Jim had, as was customary, provided a lovely rehearsal dinner and the organist, Dorothy, had invited some of the young people to come and sing for the entertainment. It had been an enjoyable evening, but Josie was tired and ready to leave. However, everyone else seemed to be happily visiting with no signs of ending the evening.

"Josie?" Pamela came over to her daughter and put an arm around her. "Are you okay?"

"I'm just tired, Mom. I don't know why."

"I'm sure some of it is emotional fatigue. This is a very special time for you but it's also a time of great change. Even good changes can be stressful. Plus, you and Scott have been moving your things into the house so you're physically tired, as well."

"I am grateful that Patrick will walk me down the aisle tomorrow. He's a wonderful man and I'm lucky to have him for a stepdad. But I had hoped Dad would change his mind and come. It just doesn't seem right for him to not give me away."

"I know it's disappointing for you. Frankly, I'm surprised that Sam didn't change his mind and come. I can't imagine him missing your wedding."

"Me, either."

"Josie?" Scott was at her side. "What's wrong?"

"I'm just tired, Scott," Josie said.

"That's not all, Josie. Tell him," Pamela urged. "It's important that you are honest with each other about your feelings and your hurts."

"I'm disappointed that Dad didn't change his mind and come. I've always thought he'd give me away some day. It just doesn't seem right that he won't even be here."

Scott put his arm around Josie and leaned down to drop a quick kiss on her lips. "I'm sorry, too. I know how much it means to you."

Hope joined them. "What's up, Josie? You getting all weepy eyed because the wedding's tomorrow? Changing your mind?" She smiled.

Pamela took Hope's arm and started walking away, explaining Josie's disappointment and fatigue.

"You look tired, Josie. Do you want me to take you home? For the last time?" He grinned at her. "After tomorrow, I'll never have to do that again."

"Do you think it would be okay for us to leave? I really am tired, but I don't want to be rude," Josie said.

"I'll just tell Mom and then we'll leave. After all, you need your beauty sleep, I guess anyway. Right?"

SCOTT KISSED JOSIE GOODNIGHT and reluctantly prepared to leave her.

"I'll see you at the church tomorrow afternoon. Right? You're not going to back out on me, are you?"

"No, silly. But you can't see me before the wedding. It's supposed to be bad luck."

"That's ridiculous! Christians don't have luck, good or bad. God is in charge."

"I agree. But I still think we shouldn't see each other."

"It's going to be kind of hard to get married if we can't see each other," Scott protested.

"You know what I mean," Josie smiled.

Another quick kiss and Scott was on his way home and Josie was headed for her bed. I don't remember ever being this tired before, she thought. The rehearsal and dinner seemed harder than any workday I've put in for either Dad or Scott. That's crazy! But I guess it's like Mom said. It's not all physical tiredness.

Josie hopped in and took a quick shower, sat down with her Bible and read for a few minutes, reviewing the scriptures PJ was going to use in the ceremony and re-reading the love chapter in Corinthians. Kneeling by her bed she prayed, then climbed wearily into bed. Her last night to sleep here in this place. Alone.

Tomorrow night she would be a married woman and she and Scott would be someplace she didn't even know about. They were taking a few days for a honeymoon, but Scott was keeping their destination a secret. She didn't even know if they were driving somewhere or flying. She'd never flown before so had mixed feelings about that. Oh, well. Anywhere with Scott would be lovely.

She drifted off to sleep with thoughts of Scott, the wedding, Sam, and everyone else skipping through her mind.

JOSIE WOKE UP LAZILY and stretched. Hmm. Oh, goodness! This is my wedding day! I'd better get busy!

She sat straight up and swung her legs over the side of the bed. This is goofy. I don't have anything to do until noon when I get my hair done.

She laid back down and dreamily went through the wedding, as per the rehearsal. The songs they'd chosen were nice, she especially liked, 'Whither thou goest, I will go.'

It was actually Ruth speaking to her mother-in-law, Naomi, but it was a lovely sentiment for a wedding and both Scott and Josie had liked it as soon as they heard it.

The daydreaming faded as Josie realized she was hungry. I don't think I ate very much at the dinner last night, she recalled. I wonder if I'm too late for Mrs. Stewart's breakfast. Well, I can run by one of the fast food places and get something, I should think. She was pulling on her jeans as she was debating what she wanted for breakfast. By the time she had her shirt and shoes on, someone knocked on her door.

It was Scott. "Hi, gorgeous. Wanna go get some breakfast?"

"Scott! You're not supposed to see me!" But she threw her arms around his neck and lifted her head for his kiss. "How did you know I'd need to go get breakfast?"

"I figured, as tired as you were last night, you might not wake up in time for the breakfast here."

"Smart guy. I figured I'd just run by and get something at a drive through window."

"We could do that. Or we could take our time someplace. How much time do you have?"

"I have to get my hair fixed at noon," Josie replied.

"Okay. Let's go have breakfast somewhere so we can just sit and relax for a while. I don't think we'll have much time for that for the rest of the day."

"Sounds great. Some time with you sounds even better." Josie grabbed her keys and bag and preceded Scott down the steps. As they ate their leisurely breakfast, Scott asked Josie something she'd left hanging quite some time back.

"Okay, tell me about the one time you used the blackmail material against Hope," he asked.

"I did what?"

Scott reminded her of her story about Hope messing up in her soccer game because the goalkeeper from the boys' team showed up and then Hope forging a note from Sam to excuse her from school the next day.

"Oh, yeah." Josie was clearly not anxious to explain.

"Josie, what's the deal?"

"Oh, it just turned out badly. Hope was a sophomore and I was in 8th grade. I'd gotten cornered into taking a babysitting job down the street and I didn't want to do it. I tried to get Hope to go but she refused until I threatened to tell Dad she'd forged his name. She went. But it turned out to be a lousy evening for everyone concerned and I've always felt guilty for making her be there."

"What happened?"

"The dad got mad and left his wife at a party and started home by himself. He was drunk and caused an accident that killed someone else we knew. By the time they found the mom and got her home to the kids, Hope was getting frantic. Her best friend had called to say her little brother had been killed in an accident and Hope couldn't leave the kids to go be with her friend."

"But you couldn't have known something so horrible would happen," Scott insisted. "It wasn't your fault."

"No, but if I'd gone ahead and babysat, Hope would have been able to go to her friend. If I'd even stayed home, I could have gone to relieve Hope so she could leave. But I'd gone over to a friend's house to spend the night."

"Couldn't they have called you there?" Scott asked.

"Should have been able to," Josie agreed. "But, for some reason, Dad insisted he couldn't find the phone number. So, I didn't learn about it until the next morning when I came home. It's just always been a touchy subject for me and for Hope."

"Well, then, I'm sorry I asked," Scott apologized.

"No problem. But could we talk about something else now?"

They started talking about the fall and winter and all they'd done since they'd started going out together. They were soon laughing, and Josie was much more relaxed.

Scott deposited Josie back at the rooming house just in time for her to get in her truck and drive to the hair salon where she was having her hair done. Hope and Cindy were meeting her there so they could all get 'purty together' as they put it. When the other two found out that Josie and Scott had been together for the morning they were horrified.

"Josie! He's not supposed to see you before the wedding!"

"Oh, that just means he shouldn't see me in my gown before the ceremony," she said nonchalantly, grinning from ear to ear. "Besides, we don't believe in luck."

Their hairdressers finally seated the girls and the serious business at hand became their priority. They each knew about what they wanted their hair to look like but were a bit vague on the details. But by the time they left to go to the church to get dressed, they all three looked lovely, at least to each other.

JOSIE KEPT PEEKING OUT the door of the dressing room, trying to see who all was at the church for the wedding, although, this early, only the wedding party was arriving. Hope would pull her back from the door, shut it and then scold her. "Honestly, Josie. Can't you behave yourself for once!"

Josie's moods swung from total elation to fear to sorrow and back to joy. She was happy to be marrying Scott, happy her mother was there, a little afraid of the lifetime commitment she was about to make, and sad that Sam wasn't there to be a part of it.

Barb and Pamela arrived about an hour before the ceremony was scheduled to begin and started bustling around checking on the cake, the flowers, the little bags of seeds, the ribbons on the ends of the pews, and anything else either of them thought of. They were having the time of their lives and their smiles were contagious. The organist and soloist came in early to go through the music one last time and the photographer was knocking on doors, wanting to get the shoot started.

As they gathered in the front inside the church to pose for the pictures they would always treasure, Josie couldn't keep her eyes off Scott. He looks SO handsome! She giggled as Hope whispered in her ear, "He sure cleans up good!"

Scott was having a hard time not just staring at Josie. Wow! She's beautiful! I'm so lucky. Oops, I almost forgot. We don't believe in luck.

Okay then, I'm very fortunate! He grinned to himself then caught Josie looking at him. He smiled at her, touched his fingers to his lips and blew the kiss to her.

The photographer arranged them, took pictures, rearranged them, took more pictures and then repeated it again. They were all getting tired of the posing and were glad when he finally dismissed them. He would shoot during the wedding, also, of course but the posed pictures are a large portion of the total package.

Finally, everyone was ready, and the church was filling up quickly.

Scott came and escorted Barb up the aisle and seated her with Jim, after kissing her gently. Eric was allowed to escort Pamela to her seat and then he and Scott joined Terry, Tim, and the minister up front.

The music began and Andi walked slowly up the aisle and met Eric and they took their places. Then Cindy walked up to join Tim and Hope made her way to the front to join Terry. All eyes were on the back of the church and the organist started the Wedding processional and everyone stood.

Josie was coming out of the dressing room to join Patrick for the long walk up the aisle when she heard the door of the church open. It was Sam.

Josie flew to him and threw her arms around him. "Dad! I'm so glad you came!"

"Am I too late?"

"No. You're right on time. Come on in. It's time to go."

Patrick joined them and Josie introduced the two men. Patrick said, "I'll go join your mom now, Josie. Sam is here to walk you down the aisle."

But Josie held him back. "No, Patrick. Don't go, please. Can I have you both walk me down the aisle and give me away?" she pleaded.

So, after a short delay, Josie started up the aisle, flanked by Patrick and Sam and wearing the largest smile Scott had ever seen on her. He smiled his approval.

As Pamela realized what was happening, tears of joy, for Josie, streamed down her face. Barb looked to her, questioningly, and Pamela nodded her head and mouthed, 'it's her dad'. Barb understood and whispered to Jim. They watched Scott's face of joy and saw Josie's happiness and quietly said, "Thank you, Father. You are so good."

The ceremony was lovely and the music beautiful, but all Scott and Josie could see and hear was each other. At the conclusion of the ceremony, PJ said, "Let me introduce you to Mr. & Mrs. Scott Mayforth."

Scott firmly took Josie's arm and they walked, almost ran, to the rear of the church and stole a quick kiss before their attendants joined them for the reception line. The parents joined them and there was some confusion as to where Sam should stand. Patrick pulled Sam in on the other side of Pamela and said, "Can you two get along for a little while for Josie?"

Sam looked at Pamela and said, "I'm so sorry. Can you forgive me?"

Pamela kissed him on the cheek and said, "I already have. Isn't our daughter beautiful?"

Everyone breathed a sigh of relief and the ushers started the long line of well-wishers toward the back of the church. Josie and Hope exchanged smiles, then a quick hug. Scott said, "Okay, ladies. Here come all those lovely people who came to get us off to a good start. Let's be sure they have a nice time."

They did.

THE END

www.ingramcontent.com/pod-product-compliance
Lightning Source LLC
Chambersburg PA
CBHW070040030726
47506CB00003B/809